On Mermaid Avenue

ON

MERMAID

AVENUE

by Binnie Kirshenbaum

Fromm International Publishing Corporation
New York

Published in 1992 by Fromm International
Publishing Corporation,
560 Lexington Avenue, New York, NY 10022

Manufactured in the United States of America

Printed on acid-free paper

First Edition 1992

Library of Congress Cataloging-in-Publication Data

Kirshenbaum, Binnie.
On Mermaid Avenue / by Binnie Kirshenbaum. — 1st ed.
p.   cm.
ISBN 0-88064-139-8 (acid-free paper) : $15.00
I. Title.
PS3561.I77505   1993
813'.54—dc20   92-23224
                                                    CIP

for Susan, of course

CONTENTS

PROLOGUE

The best wedding I ever went to was Louise Crane's. It did not promise to be a fine wedding. Louise was something of a drip, and picking the hottest day of the century for a wedding was none too bright either. It was so damn hot I almost didn't go, which would've been a shame as it turned out to be a splendid wedding. When I called Edie and said, "I'm not going. It's too damn hot," Edie said, "But that's why you must go. We'll faint from this heat and cause a commotion. I just love it when girls swoon from the heat. It's so delicate of us. Don't you just love it when girls swoon? You have to go, Monarose, because I won't swoon if you don't."

So I took another shower and slipped on a flimsy

dress that kept falling off my shoulders. Not exactly appropriate for a wedding, but it was a breezy dress and my date thought I looked swell in it.

My date called for me in a rented yellow Datsun with a busted air conditioner. By the time we got across town to fetch Edie and her date, I was sticking to the plastic upholstery. I loathe sticking to car seats, so I squirmed and fussed and blamed the humidity on Louise Crane and my date equally.

Edie was wearing less than I was, a strapless peek-a-boo frock and gold sandals. The boys loosened their ties, pulling the knots to mid-chest and opening their top collar buttons. The four of us drove to Connecticut, Edie hanging her head out the window like a dog. I fiddled with the radio, which worked about as well as the air conditioner, and said, "Let's steer this car into the first cool place we find and spend the day with tall gin and tonics. It's the only sensible thing to do."

Weddings are not sensible. Weddings, big shindigs in particular, are absurd and often ugly. Music at weddings is never music you care to dance to. You get snappier tunes on an elevator ride. Wedding feasts tend to taste like kibble, and women wearing too much perfume snatch up the centerpieces, spray-painted carnations set in Styrofoam, to take home. If this is supposed to be the biggest day in a girl's life, it doesn't leave her much to look forward to.

Edie once calculated that the average wedding costs more than the Around-the-World Excursion offered by British Air. The way it's said about a young person taking his own life, Edie said, "The waste. The terrible, terrible waste." In our own way, Edie and I were practical girls.

Louise Crane, however, wasn't at all like Edie and me. Louise was putting on a social whirl of a wedding, going so far as to hire a wedding steward. Louise claimed she needed professional organization. "You have no idea what's involved," she told us. "Choose invitations. Write up a guest list. Scheme the color. Plan the menu. Weave a theme. Hire a band. Send announcements to the *Times*. Order liquor, the flowers. There are a thousand details to a successful wedding. And that's not counting the big surprise."

Edie asked what surprise, but Louise hugged herself with her secret. "If I told you, then it wouldn't be a surprise, would it? All I'll say is mine will be the most memorable wedding of the season." Then having some idea Edie and I would be impressed, Louise let drop the cost per plate.

"All that money to have us there," Edie whispered to me, "and we don't even like her."

Later, I asked Edie if she thought Louise's surprise might be one we'd like. Edie doubted it. "Did you get a close look at that boy she's marrying? He looks like a slab of blue cheese. Such a boy is evidence to me Louise knows nothing of a good time."

The wedding, service and reception, was held in a backyard tent. A robin's-egg-blue-and-white striped tent, the same shade of blue as the bridesmaids' dresses and many of the hors d'oeuvres. The rear section of the tent was fashioned to look like a church. A makeshift altar was

set before rows of folding chairs. An aisle cut clean between the blue chairs and the white ones. "It's like a
color-coordinated revival meeting," Edie noted.

The front of the tent housed the bar and the buffet,
and too many guests were crowded around. "As long as
the Cranes have all this property," I asked, "why not have
a wedding al fresco? It's stuffy as hell in here."

The tent ceiling, the one in view, was fake, a second
canvas suspended a few feet below the real big top. At
the close of the ceremony, when the bride and groom
puckered up like a pair of goldfish in a bowl, the fake
ceiling was drawn open. It was supposed to release blue-
and-white confetti, blue balloons, and white doves. Two
dozen white doves were supposed to flap around the tent
as balloons and confetti floated to the ground. That
might've been a pretty sight had the doves not suffocated
in that narrow space of hot air. Dead doves are dead
weight, and they fell with a thud on the wedding. Dead
doves look a lot like dead pigeons.

The tent cleared out in a flash. The balloons drifted.
Louise went mad.

Even though we didn't get fed because some doves
had landed in the food, and we had to eat at a Howard
Johnson's along the Interstate, Louise Crane's wedding
was an event worth attending.

"That was enough," Edie said as she bit into a grilled
cheese sandwich, "to almost make a girl fond of Louise.
I'd be fond of her if I thought she planned it that way.
But she didn't. I could tell."

"They had to give her a sedative," I said.

"Oh, the poor thing." No one could say, "the poor thing," and not mean it the way Edie could. I got hiccups from laughing too hard. My date tried to scare the hiccups out of me, but I didn't scare easy.

Just a few days ago I asked Edie, "Remember Louise Crane's wedding? Wasn't that the best wedding ever? No one will ever top that. No one should even try."

"It must've been awful for her," Edie said.

To which I said, "Worse for the doves, I imagine."

I have another wedding to go to tomorrow. Today, really, as it's already well past midnight. Edie's wedding.

ROMANTIC LIT.

1

Edie and I should've met elsewhere, under different circumstances. Maybe while trekking from opposite directions across the Sahara. But as it happened, our introduction wasn't glamorous. After a Humanities lecture she came over to me, and as if she'd planned on making something of it, asked me my name.

I'd seen her around. You couldn't miss her. She made sure of that. She wasn't at all like anyone I knew. The girls I knew, carbon copies of their own mothers, dressed in matching Lord & Taylor outfits. This girl wore a plaid skirt, knee socks, purple spiked heels, a leather motorcycle jacket. The thick eyeliner she sported didn't blend well with her Louis Vuitton purse. Her hair, long and curled demurely at the ends, was dyed raven black. She was everything I wanted to be.

"Mona Rose," I introduced myself warily.

"Monarose," she drawled, making it one word. "Monarose," she repeated. "What a charming name."

I explained it wasn't one name. "I'm not hyphenated, nor am I like MaryAnn. Rose is my last name. I'm called Mona."

"Maybe you *were* called Mona," she said, "and not that Mona isn't a nice name, it's a very nice name, but Monarose is a flower of a name. Wouldn't you rather have a name like Monarose?"

Yes, in fact, I would've rather had a name like Monarose had I thought of it.

"I'm Edie Hawkes," she said. "But I imagine you already know that. I'm thrilled to finally meet you. All semester long I've been crazed with wonder. Who is that beautiful girl, and why doesn't she ever say a word? You're very mysterious. I know you're not shy. You're up to something. Oh," she held up a hand, "don't tell me what it is. I'd much rather learn it along the way. Or tell me a lie. A good lie is more revealing than the truth could ever be, don't you think? So, Monarose, where do you usually have lunch?"

Chock Full O' Nuts on Broadway, where I sat by myself and ate a tuna sandwich that came wrapped in wax paper, didn't quite gel with the image of the mystery woman she'd conjured up for me, so I said, "Around."

"I lunch in the Johnson Hall cafeteria," she told me. "You'll like it there. Cafeterias are elegant."

8

We stood in the cafeteria line. Edie put two bowls of red Jell-O on her tray and turned to me. "You're not a virgin, are you?"

No, but just barely, was the honest answer, but it wouldn't be the one I'd give. "No way," I said.

"Good. I can't stand a virgin. Girls ought to be promiscuous. I've already lost count of how many boys I've been to bed with. I have a reputation," she said proudly.

"Really?" I wasn't sure what to make of this. I'd been schooled to believe a reputation was to be avoided, like bad breath. Yet, I couldn't imagine a gaggle of girls standing in a bathroom gossiping about Edie. Or if they did, that she'd care.

"Well, not exactly," she admitted. "I haven't lost count. I've had seven, but I'm almost into double digits. Promiscuity is divine, don't you agree?"

Promiscuous. I mulled it over. I could manage it. That one time I had sex, I liked it very much. I could do it often.

While Edie ate her Jell-O, I experienced a sensation akin to falling in love. I wanted her for my friend, my best friend, desperately. She could rescue me, save me from a life no different from the one I'd always known.

For the rest of the day she stuck with me. By dinner time, I understood now that Edie and I had hooked up, we would, indeed, stay that way. And I tingled from the joy of anticipation.

Edie picked her classes the way she'd play the ponies. "I like the name. Romantic Lit.," she sighed as if it were all too dreamy. "Romance, Monarose. How could we go wrong with a class on romance?"

"Romantic Lit. doesn't have anything to do with romance as we know it." I tossed the course catalogue to Edie, who was sitting crosslegged on her bed, but I overshot and caught Liz Rogan in the face as she opened Edie's door to come in.

Liz Rogan was a big girl, not fat, but big the way Russian women who fought at the front were big, except Liz hadn't any pride or fury. What she did have was terrible hair, which if left alone would've been brown and frizzy. Instead, it had a copper cast and fit like a helmet.

"We're on our way out, Liz," Edie said. "Monarose and I are going for coffee."

"To discuss our options," I piped in, "because we don't want to make any rash decisions."

"What's wrong with a rash decision?" Edie asked.

Not that a bottomless cup of coffee for 50 cents wasn't a deal in our book, but Edie and I frequented the Hungarian Pastry Shop because of its name. Although the decor was chintzy yellow, whereas we believed cafés in Hungary were draped in scarlets and threadbare brocades like funeral parlors and bordellos, the words *Hungarian Pastry Shop* allowed us to pretend we were someplace else.

We took off our jackets, placed orders, lit cigarettes,

sprawled out. "Look," I nodded to my left, "there's that boy I'm in love with." He was sitting at a table by himself. I'd been in love with him for two solid weeks, although I'd only seen him around three or four times.

Edie conked herself on the head. "How could I have forgotten to tell you? I got scoop on him. He's in the School for International Affairs." Edie'd gotten this scoop at a party over the weekend.

"He was there? At the party?" I was sick at having missed such an opportunity.

"Only briefly. He left early." Edie didn't get to talk to him directly but did corner a friend of his for information.

When I'd known Edie less than a few days, she made a big deal of introducing me to a Henry Cosgrove. According to Edie, he was a lovesick puppy. "It's killing him that I know you and he doesn't," she said in a way that I was to understand this was something of a joke on Henry Cosgrove. Edie agreed to let him meet me provided Henry buy us both lunch. He also invited us to a party he was giving.

"Maybe I'll come," Edie yawned. "But Monarose go to your party? Monarose has better things to do than go to your little party."

I didn't really have anything better to do, but I played along because Edie was weaving me a legend. She was making me fabulously popular and sophisticated, too much for mere schoolboys. Such a fabrication delighted me, and so I picked up a thread and said, "Thank you for asking. It was sweet of you. Perhaps some other time."

11

The boy from the School of International Affairs was intent on his reading. "So," I asked Edie, "what else did you find out about him?"

Edie shrugged. "What else is there? He's going to be a diplomat. You're going to be a diplomat's wife. Show some enthusiasm, Monarose. Don't you realize what this means? You're going to live abroad, go to parties with political big cheeses and royalty. You will invite me to stay, won't you? There will be a spare room for me at the embassy?"

Before shopping for coronation dresses, I thought I ought to at least meet this boy. I was still caught up in some conventions. Edie, however, thought our first priority was to figure out what it will be like at the embassy after she arrives. "We'll travel a lot. Departing from railway stations dressed in Chanel suits, fur stoles draped over our shoulders. We'll carry hat boxes. Can't you picture us gadding about the continents with steamer trunks? Steamer trunks are a lost art worth reviving."

"Aren't steamer trunks kind of heavy to carry?" I asked.

"Monarose, the embassy gives you people to do that."

"Oh, I didn't know."

"Where do you think he'll be stationed? I'll bet they send him to Egypt."

Egypt was not arbitrary, not plucked from the globe at random. A boy named George, who Edie met in the laundry room, told her she looked as if she'd stepped right out of an Egyptian fresco. Edie was so taken with this compliment, she never found out why George was sitting on the floor staring into an empty dryer with no apparent business in the laundry room. Ever since then, she'd been carrying on about seeing the pyramids before she died.

"Now can I find out his name? I'll have to know his name, Edie. Suppose his name is Donald or Ronald." It had been our, thus far, combined experience that boys with those names were wretched in bed. Here it was, barely a year of being Edie's friend, and I was already seasoned. Firsthand, I knew some Dons and Rons who, inexplicably, came on contact.

"So you'll call him something else."

"But what about when I telephone the embassy to speak to my husband. I'll have to give the receptionist a name. And suppose I want to name our first-born son after him, and then discover his name is Martin. I don't like the name Martin for a child."

"Martin," Edie said, "is a good name for a cat. Besides, Monarose, you don't want children. There's nothing like a baby to ruin a girl's figure."

Never before had I heard such a thing about babies, that we might not want to have any of them. I felt a burden, one I didn't know was with me, go poof. I smiled and asked, "But what if he doesn't love me back?"

That my love for this boy go unrequited was an invented worry. "All the boys want you," Edie said. A real worry was what the Egyptian climate might do to our hair. "It could dry it out something fierce. We'll need hot oil treatments."

I cupped my hands in my chin and leaned into the current, carried along further than I ever dared to dream with Edie's talk of camels and weekends in Alexandria. How generous of her to take me with her on this adventure.

"We'll spend Sunday afternoons boating on the Nile," Edie promised me. "The Nile, you know, is deep blue and lined with palm trees."

Although I'd heard the Nile was a cesspool, that was what was so fantastic about being friends with Edie. If we wanted to drink the Nile waters, then we would not consider the possibility of contamination. And that was that.

"And did you know, Monarose, the moon over Cairo is always full?" Edie said.

See, my point exactly. Before knowing Edie I'd have assumed the moon over Cairo went through the same phases it did everywhere else. I needed her to tell me such things because I didn't have her imagination. I tended to see things more as they were, but with Edie at my side I could say, "Yes, I've heard that."

"Isn't life going to be grand?" Edie wanted to know.

"Yes," I said, "yes," as the boy I loved gathered up his books and left the Hungarian Pastry Shop without so much as a glance in my direction.

Tuberculosis was the disease of the Romantic poets, and Edie was desperate to contract it. "Think about it, Monarose. First I'd get beautiful. My cheeks would grow rosy, and the light in my eyes would dance like a moth at a flame. My hair would become lustrous. I could be in a Prell commercial."

14

"But then you'd die," I reminded her.

"So what?" Edie said.

However, once the lecture on tuberculosis was done with, Romantic Lit. went downhill fast. "Who picked this class?" Edie demanded.

"You did."

"I did? I'm disillusioned."

"Yeah, well," I said, "it's the season for that." Getting a date with my diplomat-in-training was a snap. Edie was right. All I had to do was ask. But the date fell way short of expectations, like oranges from a tree after a frost— cold, wizened little nuggets of disappointment.

"Not all of us in International Affairs want to be diplomats," he'd said.

"But you do," I insisted.

"No." He had some petty ambition, something to do with imports and exports.

"Can I see you again?" He shook my hand good-night.

Edie and I had made a rule: If we didn't want to have sex with a boy before the end of the first date, there wouldn't be a second date. What would be the purpose? So I said, "Call me when you get to Cairo. Not before."

The very next day Edie found me someone new to love. "Him," she said.

"Professor Vicars?" I didn't think I wanted to be in love with our Classics professor. It seemed commonplace. "I don't know. Students and professors. It's been done a thousand times before."

15

"Not with him, it hasn't. Other co-eds don't have your perception, Monarose. They go for the flashy professors."

We moved our seats and sat in the front row, center. Had Harrison Vicars not lectured with his nose to the podium, he would've seen a pair of girls, legs crossed, in an otherwise empty first row, giggling over his socks.

"They've got little llamas on them," Edie whispered.

I passed Edie a note: *They're not llamas. They're clocks.*

"Llamas, clocks. What's the difference? Are those not the silliest clocks you've ever seen?"

I dipped my notebook for Edie to read what I'd written: *So what if he dresses awful? I adore him.*

At the end of the hour, we shuffled around to gawk at him some more. "You have to marry him, Monarose," Edie said. "To dress him up properly. You could dress him up just darling. You've got that knack."

We stepped outside into the cold. "How do we know he isn't already married?" I buttoned up my coat.

"He's not married," Edie said. "No wife would let her husband out dressed like that."

His sports jacket was a hideous herringbone; it might even have been polyester. Still, he could've been married, and his wife just not the doting sort.

"Then such a wife deserves to lose him," Edie meted out justice as Dr. Vicars crossed our path. "You'd never let him out wearing socks with llamas on them."

I elbowed her hard because I was sure he'd heard.

16

He headed toward the library. Edie had to go along with my suggestion we tail him because for the last six nights I'd gone with her to stake out George.

George started out being nothing more than a pest, haunting the laundry room for Edie, appearing at her side from what seemed to be thin air, mooning over her. His devotion was cute. Plus, he was clever. "Admit it, Edie," I said. "Comparing you to an Egyptian fresco is pretty original."

"No it's not," she said. "I do look like an Egyptian queen. It's obvious."

On their first date, George and Edie went to a movie. He bought her buttered popcorn. He walked her home, kissed her on the cheek. It was a no-frills date. Edie said she'd go out with him again if she had nothing better to do. "He is pretty smart," she told me. "He speaks about a dozen languages."

The next time George took Edie out, he picked her up in a battered Camaro and drove her back and forth across the Manhattan Bridge, getting on and off for five hours. When that date was over, Edie was mad for him.

Something about George was off. He bore an uncanny resemblance to that actor Peter Finch, and George's hair was prematurely gray. Or maybe his hair was fine, but his face was unnaturally young. I teased Edie and said George learned so many languages because someday he'd need to speak with all earthlings. Also, George refused to tell us where he lived. He didn't refuse to give an address. He gave lots of them, only they turned out to be St. John the Divine, the Chrysler Building, a park bench adjacent to the Central Park Kiddie Zoo.

"I thought he was a regular guy. Popcorn and the movies. The most normal date I'd ever been on," Edie wailed. "He tricked me. He waited until I was in love before letting me know he was insane."

I did not remind her that it was the date on the bridge which captured her affections. Not a normal date. No movies. No popcorn.

We must've dawdled too long because when we got to the library, Dr. Vicars was nowhere in sight. So Edie and I left and turned down Broadway. "I don't know." I was losing my enthusiasm. "I'd make a lousy faculty wife. I can't type. And I can't imagine serving tea to other faculty wives."

"He's not after some tweedy, efficient wife, Monarose. He wants Aphrodite. Haven't you noticed how he lights up whenever he mentions her?" Edie suggested I wrap myself up in a sheet, weave twigs in my hair—one of those wreaths Greek goddesses sported—and march into his office. She could not have been serious, so I said, "I don't know about the sheet. White's not my color."

Edie stepped back and studied me. "Maybe you're right. We'll have to come up with something else."

A plane flew overhead. We watched it ascend, climb higher into the sky until it was lost in the purple dusk of the winter afternoon. "Is George human," Edie asked, "or have I fallen in love with an extraterrestrial who modeled himself after an actor? You'd think he could've at least made himself look like a young Gregory Peck or Warren Beatty. Who would choose to look like Peter Finch?"

"You know how aliens get the nuances wrong. He knew what humans looked like but didn't appreciate the ideals."

"Suppose George and I got married," Edie wanted to know, "and we had children . . ."

"Children?" I broke in and echoed her sentiments, "Children would ruin your figure."

"Hypothetically," she clarified. "What would our children look like?"

"Amphibians," I said, and I stopped at the fruit stand on the corner. Plucking one banana from a bunch, I paid the man who stood guard, and with flourish I peeled it. "Watch this," I instructed. I opened my mouth wide. As if I were a sword swallower at the circus, the banana slid down my throat. I pulled it out without a mark on it.

"Who taught you to do that?" Edie asked.

"Practice," I grinned.

"I'm jealous," Edie said. "You give better head than I do." Edie was not without a competitive streak. She darted to the fruit stand and returned with a small banana. "It's my first," she demurred. Edie dropped the peel to the pavement. It spread like flower petals the way banana peels do when they're props in slapstick routines.

Edie's banana broke off in the middle. She mangled it and left teeth marks, too. "Does this mean I'm not a sex kitten?" she pouted.

"Oh, Edie. It's taken me three weeks and four boys to master that. You're too impatient."

19

"You're right. Come on."

We crossed 111th Street and passed Golden Chicken. No one, absolutely no one, except very naive freshmen, ate at Golden Chicken. Their chickens died from cancer and sometimes weren't chickens at all. I had no reason to look in the window. It was just a mindless glance.

I went back for a double take. Harrison Vicars was in Golden Chicken! My Harry, at a window-side table, no less. I grabbed Edie by the wrist, yanking her into the next doorway.

"What are you doing? What's the matter?"

"He's in there, Edie. Eating. He's eating in there." I pointed off in the general direction of Golden Chicken.

Edie went to the window. She pressed her face to the glass and said, "Well, I'll be damned."

I came and stood next to her. Side by side, we gaped at Dr. Vicars eating two legs and a breast. "Doesn't he have nice table manners?" Edie remarked.

"No one eats at Golden Chicken," I said. "How could he?"

"It's that wife of his. Imagine forcing that dear man to do something as pitiful as taking his meals at Golden Chicken, a paper napkin spread across his lap."

"Let's go in there," I suggested. "Like we fell in from the heavens."

Edie vetoed that idea. "Not you. It's not fitting. He knows he's not going to find Aphrodite at Golden Chicken. All the others, maybe. But not her."

We stayed, then, on the outside looking in. When he got up to pay his bill, I took Edie by the sleeve, and we ran back along Broadway. Somehow, I saw our hair flapping behind us, as if I'd stepped out of the moment and was looking at a picture.

It was a few blocks before we stopped to catch our breath. "You don't believe days like this will ever end, do you?" Edie asked. "You think we'll always be peeking into windows watching the men we adore eating Golden Chicken? Do you think it will always be like this, Monarose?"

Edie slid into the booth across from me. Her face was puffy, her eyes two mean little slits.

"Would you care to tell me what's going on?" I asked.

Edie reached over and took one of my cigarettes. "Liz Rogan is having a crisis," Edie said. "And she expects me to do something about it." Camped out on Edie's floor, Liz was seeking comfort. "She's whining, begging me to hug her. And pat her. Imagine patting her. With that head of hair. She irons it to go like that." Edie blew a perfect smoke ring and watched it float off, a celestial inner tube she wished to climb aboard. "It's my room," Edie said. "All night she sat there heaving and sobbing in full view no matter which way I turned. You know that room of mine is only so big," Edie distanced two inches between her thumb and index finger. "I can't take another minute of her going on about how she needs me, how I'm her best friend, while I'm trying to listen to records. How'd I get to be her best friend? I'm not up to the responsibility."

Such a comment unsettled me. Suppose my friendship with Edie were temporary? Suppose she were like Mary Poppins or Pippi Longstocking, dropping in on my life, making it sparkle, but then vanishing, leaving me back where I started? How wretched it would be to return to my mundane ways after knowing the alternatives.

Edie ground out her cigarette and said, "She could at least try to buy my affections, give me money or cigarettes, but she expects me to be her friend for free."

We snuck peeks at one another, aware of the enormity of possibilities this conversation held. We risked some declaration which could prove embarrassing, or a denial that could come true. Wisely, Edie broke the mood and said, "If I ever have a breakdown, I hope I'll have the decency to go completely insane and get carted off in one of those jackets with no arms."

"At least in those jackets with no arms, you can't hug anyone."

"Oh, Monarose, you do understand." Another thing Edie wanted me to understand was that she'd called Liz Rogan's parents. Without identifying herself, Edie told the Rogans their daughter was cracking up. They'd better come get her. "Now don't look at me like that, Monarose. I had no choice. I couldn't let the girl suffer."

Edie glanced up at the grease-specked clock on the wall. It was just after four. "If they flew down from Buffalo, they ought to be picking Liz off of my floor right about now."

I lit two cigarettes and passed her one.

"Remember the first time I called you up?" Edie

mused. "And I said, 'This is Edie,' and you said, 'Edie who?'"

"I was sleeping. I've told you that countless times," I explained once more. "It was three in the morning. You woke me. I was groggy."

"I almost hung up," Edie said. "But I knew if I did, I'd never call back. Not ever."

I signaled the waiter for more coffee. Along with the pot, he brought George. It was uncanny how George could always find us, yet as much as we looked, we could never find him.

"What a nice surprise." Edie patted the seat next to her. "Sit here, George. Why, look who's here, Monarose. My very own George. My precious George."

George sat close to Edie, and they got gooey with each other, so I said, "I think I'll be off now."

"Oh, don't leave, Monarose," Edie said but only for form.

I insisted I had to study, and we let it go at that.

George had generously offered to tutor Edie in Chemistry. "How about tonight?" George asked. "Around ten?" Edie said yes, yes, although she didn't need tutoring, and, as far as we knew, Chemistry wasn't a subject George was familiar with.

"It's a code word," Edie said. "Chemistry, get it?" Edie prettied herself up in a dress that would fall away without having to tug or fumble with buttons. She didn't bother to put on underwear but did put fresh sheets on her bed.

For a giggle, she opened her Chemistry text to the chapter on combustion and placed it on the pillow.

George arrived with the chime of the chapel bells striking ten. He brought Edie candy. Loose sourballs in a baggie.

"So," Edie finished telling me the story as we walked to St. Luke's Hospital. "We talked for a while, sipped cognac, and then we smooched a bit. We smooched a bit more. I slipped out of my dress, and he threw up."

"What?"

"You heard me," Edie shifted the bundle of twigs she carried under the crook of the arm. "He vomited."

"On you? He got sick on you? In your bed? How grisly."

"No, not on me," Edie said. "I didn't actually witness it, but he raced from my room with his hands over his mouth. When he returned, he had that smell about him. So, I asked if he were feeling better now, and could we get back to what we were doing."

George, however, refused to submit to what he called "a slimy act." That's when Edie clopped him on the ear. Hard. "That'll teach you to refuse me," she said, only George could no longer hear her.

Edie saw no alternative. "Wouldn't you have done the same thing?" she asked me. "How was I supposed to know I was going to make him deaf?"

The nurse at the reception desk checked her big book like she was Saint Peter checking an even bigger book. "Your friend is no longer with us," she said.

Edie's mouth fell open. "He's dead? I killed him?"

"No," the nurse said. "He's fine. He's gone home."

"Could you tell us where that home might be?" Edie tried pulling a fast one, but the nurse wasn't authorized to give out such information.

"These are for you." Edie put the bouquet of sticks on the nurse's desk. "I picked them myself."

Across from the hospital a brand-new red Jaguar was parked at a fire hydrant. "I hate when they do that," I said aloud.

"Don't you though?" said Edie. "Red is the wrong color for that car." Edie went to it and wondered what sort of man chose red for a Jaguar.

"Divorced," I said. "A recently divorced man."

"Divorced," she repeated. "Wouldn't it be nice if this recently divorced man fell in love with me and let me drive his car? I'll bet this baby can fly." Edie swatted at the hood.

"Forget about it," I said. "He wouldn't let you drive it no matter what."

"What sort of car do you think I'll wind up with?" Edie asked me. "You know, in the long run."

"Try to avoid a Chrysler," I said. "They're part of the package that goes with tract houses and husbands who are Shriners or Moose."

"I might like that."

"You'd hate it," I told her.

"You know what would be really sad?" Edie's eyes ignited, her smile crossed boundaries as she recounted a lousy fate. "If we ended up with the Mercedes package. The whole deal. In silver. That could happen to me. I might very well wind up in an affluent suburb, taking to drink and to Valium." Edie held out her hand for a cigarette. "You'd come as a guest to my country club and pity me, wouldn't you?"

This was too familiar for comfort. Edie was dredging up my past, and I'd never go back. Not even as Edie's guest would I return to Great Neck Country Club to sit amongst the sea of bobbed noses and frosted hair, to join in on talk of sweater sets, china patterns. "No," I told her. "I don't play golf or tennis. There's no reason for me to go to a country club."

"So you'll sit beside me at the pool," Edie said. "We'll chain-smoke and read poetry aloud. And you'll pretend not to notice that I'm drinking gin from a thermos. Gin is what you drink when you're bent on forgetting."

"That is not going to happen to you, Edie. Don't you know if you sat by the pool day after day, your skin would look like an old shoe?"

"It was a sad thought, though. Wasn't it a sad thought?" Sad thoughts were a delight which left us giddy. We could embrace such things as long as they were remote or impossible.

Edie patted the car adieu and said to me, "We're going to have all sorts of fun, aren't we? We're going to have lives worth remembering, don't you think?"

I wanted to stop Edie right there, take her by the shoulders and ask, "Aren't you having fun right now? Isn't this worth remembering? What is it you're looking for when what we've got is so sublime?" Instead, I followed

26

her down the subway steps and through the turnstile.

We stood close to the platform edge, peering down the tunnel. With her back to me, Edie asked, "What kind of car should George and I get?"

"A flying saucer? A bicycle?"

"I'm serious, Monarose."

Our train pulled in. There weren't two adjoining seats available, so we held onto the pole as the train lurched out of the station.

"I'm going to marry George." Edie's voice was flat and dry like a wafer. "I'm going to marry George because I want to. We're going to live in Gramercy Park. Our apartment will have a balcony and parquet floors. Can't you just picture that?"

"No," I said. "I can't picture George living anywhere except in another dimension." I waited for Edie to laugh, but from out of nowhere, she got quiet, the same quiet as before a hurricane or tornado, very still and dark, and you wish for some sort of noise. Such calm has a deadly ring to it. When she finally spoke, she was toneless. "I thought you were my friend."

"Of course I'm your friend."

"I never expected you to turn against me," she said, as if I had. And when the subway doors opened at 72nd Street, Edie got off.

In class I took my usual seat, but Edie went and sat way in the back. To look at her, I'd have had to shift around in my chair. I didn't run into her at lunch nor at the library. At night, I sat on my bed and waited for my phone to ring.

Another day went by, and still Edie kept her distance. I wanted so much to go to her, but if an overture were to be made, Edie would have to be the one to make it. She was the one who invented me as the ice princess, and ice princesses don't defrost for anyone; especially not those who made them so. If she hadn't so often said, "Monarose does not grovel. Not to anyone for any reason," I could've picked up with her. While I was not as apt to fly off the handle as Edie, I was supposed to be the tough one. It was possible she didn't call me because she believed I might very well reject her apology.

On the third day, I moped over to Chock Full O' Nuts, dreary with the prospect of lunch there. George was at the counter, gauze taped over his right ear. He spun around on his stool, nervous and jumpy. "She's not with you, is she?"

"I'm alone," I said. "How's the ear?"

"Better, thank you. You're sure she's not hiding someplace?" He bent down and checked beneath the counter, as if Edie were crouching there ready to pounce.

"Honest," I told him. "She's not with me. I don't know where she is." I took the stool on George's left. "We're not speaking."

"Aren't you afraid? Who knows what she'll do?" George warned me to be very, very careful. "Always check behind you. You never know when she'll attack."

"Must you constantly be strange, George? Couldn't

you let go of it for a bit? Be an average boy? You had some fun with Edie. Couldn't you be her boyfriend for a few days? She'd tire of you soon enough. It wouldn't have to be for long."

Climbing off his stool, George said, "Not even for one second."

In my mailbox, along with the Con Ed bill and a free sample of laundry detergent, was a Western Union telegram. How curious. I'd thought telegrams were defunct, on the list of things extinct like absinthe, the dodo bird, dance cards.

EVEN IF YOU DON'T LOVE ME, I STILL LOVE YOU STOP EDIE.

I read it aloud and then a few more times to myself before thumbtacking it to the wall above my desk. There I could look at it a lot and marvel that I had a friend who sent telegrams.

"Hi," I said when Edie answered her phone. "It's me."

"Oh, Monarose. I'm so relieved. Whoever thought days could be so long? I can't even recall what our fight was about. Do you recall?"

"We didn't have a fight," I said.

"Even better. It never happened." After a small pause, Edie mentioned she'd seen me at Chock Full O' Nuts. "You were sitting with George. I was standing outside, all pathetic and lonely. What did George have to say for himself?"

"Nothing much. The ear's okay. He can hear."

"Well, I suppose that's good. Did he say anything about me?"

"No. Nothing."

"Good. That's good. He came between us, Monarose. Our little tiff was because of him and his ways. We mustn't tolerate anyone coming between us. Woe to those who try."

"Yes," I said because the main thing was that we were friends again. Besides, a girl's got the right to unfold events in her own arrangement.

Not long before graduation, when priorities should've been padding résumés, going on interviews, Edie and I parked ourselves on the library steps to smoke cigarettes. Edie'd been on one interview, to be a stewardess. Flying around didn't seem like work. But she didn't get the job because she showed up at the personnel office wearing black fishnet stockings and gloves without fingers, and she gave all the wrong answers to questions asked.

"Why didn't you tell them what they wanted to hear?" I asked. "That should've been easy enough."

"They asked trick questions," Edie told me. "What are my hobbies? Do I consider myself a cheerful, good-natured person? So, I told them I didn't have hobbies. I have passions. And no, I'm not cheerful, and I don't think of myself as a person. I'm a girl."

30

"You didn't really want that job, did you?" I asked.

"I suppose not," she said. "Who'd want to work for a company that tries to trip you up on the interview?" Edie flicked her cigarette down the steps and watched it tumble. "I know this might be a dreary question, Mona-rose, but what do you think we ought to do come June?"

I ignored the obvious and said, "The first thing we have to do is get you an apartment." Living off-campus, which initially had to do with not getting my housing application in on time, turned out to be a stroke of genius, sparing me from the apartment-hunt scramble. "You can't stay on in the dorms after you graduate. You'll need a place to live."

"I meant about our careers," Edie said.

"Oh. That." I'd gone so far as to write up a skeleton of a résumé. I had it with me, tucked into a notebook. Also, I'd been to visit the people at the Placement Office. A prissy man there asked what was my field of interest. Because I hadn't a clue, he hustled me off to a brisk woman who missed her calling as the sort of nurse who collects urine samples. She gave me a series of multiple choice tests which were supposed to match me up with a career like a computer date. The boxes I checked off were the ones which read: Stay at home and read a book, Read to a sick friend, Go for a walk.

I'd have thought my responses would've qualified me to be a nursing home attendant or a poet. "Market Re-search," the woman concluded.

Edie broached the subject of careers because she'd been mulling it over for weeks and had arrived at her conclusion. "We're not qualified," she said.

"Maybe not, but we still have to get jobs."

"Oh? Really?" Edie acted as if this were news to her. "Since when don't we have the right to pursue happiness as it's guaranteed in the United States Constitution?"

"Since we have to pay for things like food and rent. Otherwise," I asked, "how will we live?"

Edie held her hand out for another cigarette and said, "We'll live off the fat of the land," as if New York were Tahiti and we could reach out a window and pluck a mango from a tree. "Face it, Monarose. We can't hold down a career and pursue happiness at the same time." Edie put forth a choice. "It's either a routine which will destroy us or the luxury of being poor."

"Poor?" I said. "*Poor* as in unable to invest heavily in the stock market and vacationing in Portugal where the dollar goes farthest? Or *poor* as in burning furniture for fuel and shopping with food stamps?"

"Not food stamps," Edie said. "Think of them as ration cards. And we'll be *poor* as in bohemian. We'll dress in tattered cast-off velvets which are daring and chic. We'll throw dinner parties and serve boiled potatoes and cheap Chianti. Poverty will stretch our imaginations. We'll transcend the experience and be rich in other ways. Poverty is only a state of mind, Monarose."

Edie said that we'd still have certain luxuries. Jewels and baubles and pretty trinkets would gravitate to us, fall into our laps like rain from the sky. "It's natural selection."

We were, for the necessities, to take part-time, temporary jobs. Coffeehouse waitresses, bookstore clerks, receptionists for shady operations.

"Suppose we don't make enough money to cover our rent? Or to buy cigarettes? To say we're poor might sound peachy, but can you really imagine scouting the pavement for a discarded Lucky Strike?" I asked.

"Don't be disgusting." For the times we'd never want to go through, despite the high volume of life experience, Edie had a back-up plan. "You know how our parents consider us irresponsible. Be honest, Monarose. You failed ceramics. A responsible person doesn't fail clay. A responsible person doesn't take clay in the first place."

I might've failed clay, but I was an amateur at irresponsibility compared to Edie. She was the professional who routinely blew her allowance on one-way plane tickets to London or Kansas City, then phoning home collect, broke and stranded.

"You know our parents are perched like vultures, waiting for us to screw up, just so they can swoop down squawking, 'I told you so.' It would be a severe shock to them if we landed careers, if we balanced our checkbooks, thus falling short of their expectations. We mustn't prove our parents wrong," Edie said. "It'd be disrespectful."

My parents were hoping I'd become a schoolteacher. Nothing fancy, but also nothing that would embarrass anyone. And only until I married and had a family anyway. I never wanted to be a schoolteacher.

"I think poverty will be divine, Monarose. What do you think?"

My experience with poverty was limited to occasionally wandering around in what my mother called "a bad area," the same neighborhoods my father would drive us through on our way to the theatre or some museum. On cue, sighting the first tenement, my mother'd warn, "Lock your door, Mona, and look how they hang their laundry on clotheslines. See how poor people have to live." My mother also made me read *Marjorie Morningstar* so I would know that, even if I rebelled and experimented with bohemian lifestyles, ultimately I'd wind up marrying a nice dentist because that's how it is for upper-middle-class Jewish girls. In the end, they don't have a choice.

"So, what's it going to be, Monarose?" Edie asked.

I took my résumé from my notebook. "I guess I won't be needing this," I said.

Edie snatched the paper from me and read it over. "Just as I suspected," she said. "No one would hire you anyway. No one could afford to." Edie folded my résumé into an airplane, a glider, and sent it flying.

INTERNATIONAL INTRIGUE

2

Edie and I were not given the graduation gifts we'd asked for. No one bought us unlimited free checking accounts, gold bricks, or large sums of cash. As if our parents had conferred on this, we both got trips abroad—one month in the country of our choice.

Although it had been ages since I had my little crush on Professor Vicars, I remained faithful to his vision of Greek gods and goddesses as a fun group who threw wild parties. I thought I'd frolic on Mount Olympus, drink nectar, eat grapes, indulge in a Dionysian frenzy or two. Edie would finally see the frescoes and the pyramids.

We scheduled our departures for the same day, so we could share a cab to the airport. We promised to miss each other fiercely until we could meet up in Alexandria.

In Athens, I discovered the gods were summering elsewhere. I got on a boat bound for Paros to hunt them down in caves and catacombs. In and out of the ruins at Rhodes, I searched. But there, too, I came up empty. If that weren't lousy enough, the Greek sun turned my hair orange and my skin martini-olive green. Greece was no place for me.

Direct from the airport, Edie came to my apartment. She was in a huff. "Where were you? I waited in Alexandria for days. We were supposed to have lunch on the Nile. I found us the perfect spot, linen tablecloths, a good wine list, and you don't show up."

I explained she wouldn't have wanted to have lunch with me. "I was green and orange, Edie. I would've clashed with the decor."

Edie thought this picture through, and agreed, yes, it was best I'd stood her up. She was sorry Greece wasn't what I'd had in mind. "Maybe we shouldn't ever visit the places we most want to go to. From now on, let's travel without forethought. To places we've never heard of. I am sorry," she repeated.

The pyramids were smaller than Edie expected, but her trip was not a bust. Egypt was crawling with frescoes. "They do look exactly like me. See for yourself." She opened her suitcase and took out reams of postcards, all of frescoes of Egyptian queens. They looked most like

Edie around the hair, especially since she'd had hers cut like Cleopatra. "And look what else I got us," Edie reached back into the suitcase. "Kohl." She held up two small glass bottles filled with black dust. Kohl was what racy women in the 1920s wore as eye makeup. I'd always imagined it like an artist's charcoal stick or as a briquette for the barbecue. "It looks like we're supposed to pinch it up our noses," I said.

The kohl was so deep of a black, it cast a blue tint to the whites of our eyes. We crowded at my mirror, and I observed, "We look beautiful."

"More beautiful," Edie amended. Then she asked, if we had to pick, would we choose to be beautiful or to be intelligent?

"You can't be one without the other," I said. "No matter how pretty, there's no beauty to a dumb girl. Nothing radiates. And smart girls are smart enough to fix themselves up right."

"I missed you," Edie said to the mirror. "What about eyeshadow with this? Would that be too much?" But before I could say maybe, Edie answered her own question. "Nah. There's never too much. There's no such thing."

We did not discuss the possibility of Edie bunking with me until she got a place of her own. Roommates are sticky business, often reducing friendships to rubble. We weren't willing to gamble.

Edie arranged to stay with Janet, a girl we knew at

school who shaved off her eyebrows because hair on a face was messy, sloppy-looking, a dust magnet. Janet had a two-bedroom apartment on the Upper West Side.

When we got to Janet's, she made us take our shoes off before we could come inside. She'd just washed her floors. I whispered to Edie, "Are you going to like living with someone who makes you take your shoes off?" Edie whispered back, "I'm not sure I'll like living with a person who washes her floors." Eyebrows were not all Janet deemed messy. Edie was messy too. "You wouldn't have believed it, Monarose. I made a cup of coffee, and she came charging at me with a coaster. A coaster. In my own place of residence, a coaster."

Janet was a squeaky-clean lunatic. Her bathroom closet was stacked with feminine hygiene products, and her kitchen cabinets stored caseloads of detergents. Edie held a disposable douche in one hand and a bottle of Mr. Clean in the other. "I know these things are connected," she said, "but I really don't want to discover how."

To get an apartment of her own, Edie was willing to make compromises. She'd pay more than she could afford and so managed to secure a place within a week. She neglected to tell Janet she was moving out, so she left behind a sink full of dirty dishes and an ashtray brimming with cigarette butts and chewing gum. "Now she won't feel bad that I've gone," Edie explained.

———

Stretched out on my divan, Edie picked pecans from the tarts her mother had sent me. The divan was a new addition to my apartment, purchased when shopping with Edie for furniture for her place. Edie pressed the day couch on me, insisting it was a prop I couldn't do without. Lounging on it, lounging on it naked and eating an apple, I'd be reminiscent of a marble statue.

I sat at my desk filing my fingernails.

"Why is it my mother sends you pecan tarts?" Edie asked. "She's *my* mother."

The tarts were Mrs. Hawkes's way of thanking me for finding Edie when she went to visit her mother but never got off the plane. Mrs. Hawkes called me in a panic. I called the airport, learned the plane made a stopover in Atlanta. As long as a city had a Hilton Hotel, it was a good bet Edie'd be at it. She favored Hiltons because Elizabeth Taylor was once married to the man who owned them. Elizabeth Taylor was an idol of Edie's because Edie admired women who married often.

I shook a bottle of nail polish and painted one hand, fanning my fingers out for Edie to see. "What do you think of this color?" I asked.

"Very Berlin-before-the-war," Edie said. Then she let go with three pained little sighs. "Oh, Monarose, why does passion have the life-span of a sneeze?"

While Edie was in Atlanta, I went out with some boy whose name escaped me. He took me to dinner. Often I wondered why the ritual is dinner first, sex after. It should be the other way around. This boy wanted to share an appetizer of baked clams. He wanted to share some thoughts. I looked at him across the table and wondered who was this boy who wouldn't let me have my own baked clams. By the end of the dinner, I wished he'd buzz off, and I went home alone. Which wasn't at all what I had planned.

"Why can't we seem to fall in love and have passion and happiness until the end of our days?" Edie wanted to know.

We could have passion and happiness until the end of our days. Just not with one man. We needed a series of men. A series of impossible or unlikely men. Perfectly nice boys bored us. To fall in love with a perfectly nice boy was a contract, an arrangement, as exciting as a nap. Passion was something we had to be willing to die for. Nice boys couldn't inspire us to lose so much as an eye. I verbalized what I'd learned from Edie and said, "Passion is like revolution. It's got to stir the depths of the soul. There must be an element of danger."

"Danger." Edie made it sound like a foreign phrase, a wonderful one that doesn't translate. "Danger," she said again and again until it took on the flavor of *delicious*.

"Take the shark," I said. "Once it settles down, quits moving for even a second, it dies. The human heart, Edie, works pretty much the same way."

"We've so much to learn from the animal kingdom," Edie noted. "But where, I ask you, do we find these boys to have passion with? They're not the ones working at Paine Webber. I know this for a fact. I've dated most of them."

It always confused me why I had to explain to Edie the ideas she'd originated, but I did what was expected of me. "It's not a question of where to find them. It's timing. Our love affairs must be doomed from the outset. Not the sort that doom later on."

"Do you think we'd be better off dating married men?" she asked.

"In a pinch, perhaps. But with married men you run the risk of them leaving their wives for you."

"But I'd like that," Edie insisted. "If he left the wife, the house, the kids, that would be a demonstration of his affection."

"If that happened," I warned, "you'd have no one to chase. You'd be stuck with somebody else's husband. You want to fall in love with the enemy." I put intrigue on a spoon and fed it to her. "The enemy."

Edie sat up. "War is so romantic." She visibly warmed to the idea. "If we were in a war, I'd fall in love with a soldier from the other side. The captain and I would meet at night in bombed-out buildings and cling to each other while artillery fell around us. A priest in hiding would marry us, and then my captain would get killed. Wouldn't that be deluxe? Hey, Monarose, is Franco dead yet?"

It took Edie all of ten seconds to unearth a war she could exploit for romance. The Cold War. "Russians are a good-looking people, aren't they?" Edie said.

The chilly standoff with the Soviet Union might not have offered the enchantment of a lost cause, nor had it the glitter of Allied spies passing information in Lisbon, but it wasn't a half-bad set of circumstances. The enemy

41

was well-defined. Our yahoo of a president did call them the evil empire, and there wasn't any risk to life and limb.

"You're so smart, Monarose. Passion and revolution are one and the same. The Soviets are a passionate people. Think of those red flags waving against the white snows of Siberia. It's enough to give me goosebumps in private places."

Most girls would've merely doted on a fantasy for a short while. Perhaps they'd dream of a faceless man in a beaver hat. Or go to see *Dr. Zhivago* three or four times in a row, winding it up with nothing more than a crush on Omar Sharif. But Edie wasn't like most girls. The very next day she beelined over to the United Nations to scout for Soviets.

She might've taken a crack at crashing in on the General Assembly had she not first gone to the gift shop. There, taped to the cash register, was a flyer announcing a meeting of the Russian Book Club. All were invited to attend.

The Soviets billed this book club as a cultural event. A New York newspaper said it was a spy network. The Soviets countered it was a peace gesture. Edie called it the opportunity of a lifetime.

Some FBI types planted out front snapped pictures of all who entered. Edie and I stopped, first checking our makeup in compact mirrors, and posed for our dossiers. "Do you think we can get copies of those photographs?" Edie asked.

"Sure," I said. "Under the Freedom of Information Act."

The cultural event at this book club meeting was a film of the harvesting of wheat, narrated in Russian without subtitles. A man sitting behind us whispered to his companion, "Brilliant minimalism, don't you agree?"

The good thing about that film was it was over in ten minutes. When the lights went up, a woman we dubbed "Natasha" invited us to the adjoining room for "discussion of cultural event."

"If anyone asks," I instructed Edie, "say it was brilliant minimalism."

But no one asked. *Discussion of cultural event* meant a party—punch bowls of pepper vodka, smoked salmon, caviar, black bread, and potato chips. Those Soviets put out a nice spread.

"Check this out, Monarose." Edie indicated a man licking a fish egg from his upper lip. "Is he not a dead ringer for Ilya Kuryakin? Remember Ilya Kuryakin, *The Man From U.N.C.L.E.?*" Edie pushed past portly dignitaries and scrawny aides and over to the man still licking his lips.

He ladled her a fresh drink from the punch bowl. I watched them talk. Edie was animated, and the man was chuckling a split second behind Edie's laughs, as if taking a cue from her. Perhaps he spoke no English.

When we left, Edie told me all about him. His name was Vladimir. He was a minor consul and lived in the Soviet compound in Riverdale. "A bus comes to take them home. Isn't that nice? Do you think I'll like living on a compound in Riverdale?" But before I could say that living on a compound is like jail, Edie said, "You know, Monarose, there are no real causes. There's only the romance of war."

The Russian Book Club met on the third Thursday of each month, like Thanksgiving. By Monday, the prospect of not seeing Vladimir for three and a half more weeks was insufferable. Edie returned to the United Nations to ferret him out.

After hanging around the lobby, she prowled the cafeteria, but Vladimir wasn't there either. Edie strayed into the men's room hoping to find him at the urinal only to be shooed out by a Portuguese delegate. Next, she went upstairs to the General Assembly, but it wasn't in session. Alone, Edie sat in the grand auditorium figuring what to do.

At Grand Central Station, Edie boarded the train to Riverdale. From there she took a car service to the Soviet compound. It was gated, and the guard wouldn't let her dally around.

But the day wasn't over, and Edie wasn't one to give up. Determined to make contact, she bought a picture postcard of lower Manhattan and sent Vladimir a note: *I'll rescue you from mediocrity. Meet me at the Statue of Liberty. Midnight. Tonight. Love, Edie.* She posted it immediately and then called me.

"Oh, Edie," I said. "You didn't. Where'd you mail it to?"

"The U.N. I would've sent it to the compound, but I couldn't figure out the address system. He should get it tomorrow. He'll be tickled pink," she laughed at the implication of the color.

"Pink, nothing," I said. "He'll be seeing white. As in Siberian work camp."

Edie wouldn't hear that. "You do think he'll meet me, don't you?"

"No," I said. "He's probably on his way back to the Soviet Union as we speak. In handcuffs." I told Edie it was likely Vladimir's mail, and especially mail from American girls, was monitored by the KGB. "Your message sounded suspiciously like he was getting ready to defect."

Edie waffled between embracing the picture of Vladimir serving a sentence of love in the gulag and refusing to believe her note would be taken seriously. "It was a postcard, Monarose. No one puts a serious message on a postcard. Anyway, he'll explain we fell in love. The KGB will understand. Everyone understands love."

I didn't want to go to the next Russian Book Club meeting. I was having a romance of my own with one of those in-a-pinch married men. On Thursday evenings his wife went to a Creative Writing Workshop at the 92nd Street Y. Also, I wasn't keen on going because I feared we'd be booted out as agitators.

"No one's shown up at your door asking questions, have they?" Edie asked. "Believe me, it's forgotten."

The featured act was a troop of Ukrainian folk dancers.

We sat in the back row where Edie had a view of Vladimir's ears. Vladimir spotted Edie, too. No matter what she said about him looking pleased to see her, the man was terrified. Throughout the performance, he twisted in his seat to look at her and then past her, as if he knew he were being watched.

"See," Edie said. "He can't stop looking at me. He's so happy I'm here, he can hardly keep still."

At "discussion of cultural event" Vladimir backed into a corner. "Please," he begged Edie, "go away from me."

"Now, you don't mean that," Edie flirted.

"I am married man," Vladimir flattened himself against the wall as if he were preparing for the firing squad. "I love my wife very much. You Americans have no morals. I am happily married man. Go away."

Edie stormed off. "Do you believe that?" she asked me. "I don't believe that one bit. You can't believe a word these Russians say. They're experts at double-talk."

I'd had enough. Between the pepper vodka and the intrigue, I had a headache that wouldn't quit. "I'm going home," I told Edie. "Are you coming?"

"No. I'm going to stick around a while longer. See if I can't decode this double-talk of theirs."

I didn't like the idea of leaving Edie there alone. There could too easily be repercussions. She must've known how I felt because she said, "Now, don't worry. I'm not going to cause an international incident."

———

The next afternoon, Edie showed up at the Wall Street restaurant where I was checking coats. That was as near to a job as a 10¢-a-dance-girl as I could get. "Come on," she said. "Let's blow. You don't want to grow old in a job like this."

"Why aren't you at work?" I asked. Edie was employed three days a week in an office where she charted lists of numbers onto a graph.

To jazz up the job, she began throwing some of the lists into the garbage can. When the supervisor picked through Edie's trash, which was a low thing to do, he held up the crumpled lists and asked, "What should I do with you?" And Edie told him, "You could fire me."

I grabbed my jacket and left the businessmen to locate their own Burberrys in the sea of beige trenchcoats. "Where to?" I asked my friend.

"How about Coney Island?" Edie suggested this to please me. For years I'd been after her to go out there and ride the Cyclone. That she'd never been on that particular roller coaster seemed all wrong.

While we waited for the D train, Edie told me I should've stayed on last night. The book club party lasted early into the morning. "It was a gas. The only crummy thing was that creepy Vladimir slinking about. What a dud he turned out to be. A grenade that didn't go off," she said. "Looked dangerous but was only a fizzle. He'll never get anywhere with that attitude. How could I have ever loved him?"

Boris, however, was another story. Boris was worthy

of Edie's attentions. Boris had to be high up on the chain of Soviet command because he was an old gentleman, and because he sought Edie out while she stood alone by the punch bowl. "He wasn't afraid of me," she said. "Boris isn't afraid of anything."

It occurred to me Boris sought Edie out to pump her, to find out what she was up to. But Edie said, "No. He was quite smitten with me. Boris is very discriminating and does as he chooses. Unlike Vladimir." Edie raised her voice over the screech of the train pulling in. "Vladimir is but a pawn in the political arena."

On a Friday afternoon in May the amusement park at Coney Island didn't do big business. There were no lines to wait on, and we got the Cyclone all to ourselves, which was like being on a ghost train.

We sat in the first car waiting for it to start up, and I explained to Edie why the Cyclone was the pinnacle of roller coasters. It may no longer be the biggest or the fastest, but it's the only one made of wood. Wood can break apart in a snap. It is that possibility which gives the Cyclone its status. Also, that second dip is a lulu.

"Look," Edie pointed upward. "I think that plank is cracked."

Slowly at first, the cars crept uphill, picking up steam along the way, until we reached sufficient height to make downhill a fright. It was on the top peak, where the cars pause to teeter, I pictured careening off the track and plunging onto Mermaid Avenue below. The pavement would magically become the sea, green and briny and deep. Edie and I would float to the bottom and ride sea horses and eat oysters. Mermaid Avenue was the prettiest name for a street. So pretty a name, I'd have lived there if it weren't such a run-down pit of a place.

We didn't wait for the cars to come to a full stop before hopping out on wobbly legs. "So," I asked Edie, "was that not a swell ride?"

Edie agreed it was well worth the trip out but felt it would've been enhanced had we not finished exactly where we'd begun. "They should let us off over there," she nodded to the other side of the park. "It ought to have a destination. All too often the good things go in circles."

On her kitchen wall, Edie had a map of the world. All the spots she'd been to were circled in red. She aimed to touch base in as many places as possible, even if only to stay a few minutes. She hoped to reduce the planet to a small, flat area where no one could go too far away, where no one was out of reach.

Although we had no intentions of eating such a product, we bought ourselves a pair of cotton candies. Pink gossamer on a paper cone is the pixiest accessory for strolling by the merry-go-round, the ferris wheel, the tilt-a-whirl. These rides, compared to the Cyclone, were woozy. We wouldn't waste our time riding on them. We despised anticlimax. "You want to walk over to Brighton Beach?" I asked Edie. "We can mingle with the Russians there." Home to a large number of Soviet émigrés, Brighton Beach was a short stretch up the boardwalk.

"Defectors, ugh." Edie was suddenly elitist about her Communists.

"You can snub the defectors," I said. "Let's walk along the boardwalk. We'll go eat a hot dog."

Dropping the cotton candies in a garbage can, we stepped up onto the tired boardwalk. It was splintered and sagging, and we left Coney Island behind us.

"You know," Edie fell into step, "I'm not sure Vladimir is even Russian. He actually told me my feelings for him weren't healthy. Sounds like American propaganda to me. Healthy," she snorted and lit a cigarette.

"Maybe he didn't mean healthy in the bean sprout way. Maybe he meant safe."

Safe was worse than healthy. "What sort of coward values safety over passion? He's a minor consul, Monarose. And he'll never amount to anything more. He lacks Russian temperament. He's nothing like Boris. You can bet Boris doesn't play it safe." Edie was off again, several paces from the ground. "Boris is dreamy. He's the one I really want. The one I was meant to have. Boris is a big cheese in the KGB."

"He told you he is in the KGB?"

"Not in so many words. He told me he was a translator whose only wish was for world peace. That's got to be KGB."

"What else did he tell you?" I asked.

"That the Politboro is made up of nice guys like George Bush."

Boris was one smart cookie. When Edie told him they'd make such a cute couple, Boris said, "Ah, Edette, what do you want with seventy-year-old Bolshevik?" First off, he wasn't a day over sixty-two. And, he knew exactly what Edie wanted. Boris was a born diplomat, never offending with pedestrian excuses. Instead, he said, "Edette, you are going to be cause of World War III." Grouping her with Helen of Troy was flattery enough to camouflage any whiff of rejection.

The park bench at Hirsh's Hot Dog and Knish stand was vacant, so we sat there. The direct sunlight warmed our faces. A group of girls walked by us. They were, give or take a year, about our age and were dressed in springtime pastels, like a box of sachets. Edie and I never wore those colors, and we never went around in a cluster. "Isn't it something we found each other?" I asked.

Edie said it would've been very sad if we hadn't, and did I want a hot dog? She got up and offered, "Let me buy my Monarose a hot dog."

In a flash she was back, empty-handed. "Why, I don't have one ruble on me," she said. "Give me some cash so I can buy my Monarose a hot dog."

HOCUS-POCUS

3

A Gypsy in a storefront beckoned us through the window, and Edie's heart set on going inside.

"She beckons everyone," I said. "It's her job."

"It's only three dollars, Monarose. For three dollars we can afford to find out what she's got to say," Edie reasoned.

We sat on the Gypsy's faded floral couch and paid her up front. She put the money down her bosom and read my palm. "You will get married soon," she told me. "To a very nice man. You will move away from here and have two . . . no, three children. One of the babies will die young." The Gypsy wiped a tear from her eye.

This Gypsy wasn't up on current events. That was my

old fortune—to marry, live in a comfortably big house, have children, become sad, know something is missing but never be able to put my finger on what, to have regrets. That was the fortune I would've had if Edie and I hadn't become friends. But that couldn't happen now. No way were we going to spend afternoons pushing baby strollers through the shopping mall. We, Edie and I, were bound for extraordinary times.

According to this Gypsy, Edie was also going to marry and have three babies. All her babies would survive. "But *who* am I going to marry?" Edie was after names and dates. That information cost five more dollars. We didn't have it.

Outside, back on the street, Edie said to me, "Three children? I'd never have three children. And did you catch how she hedged when I asked for a particular? I don't think she knew her stuff. What do you think?"

"*I'm* a better psychic than she is," I said, meaning she wasn't one at all, but Edie gave it another interpretation. "Of course you are," she insisted.

Other than plucking daisy petals to see if I were loved and being aware when the 13th fell on a Friday, I put no stock in hocus-pocus until Edie left me no choice. To aid me in delivering tomorrow's gossip today, she bought me a deck of Tarot cards and a crystal ball. I took to wearing brightly colored shawls, hoop earrings, and a turban, and honed my knack for predicting what Edie wanted to hear.

Maybe mysticism is nothing more than a door you open when you've too much time on your hands, but as long as we were messing with it, I thought a hint of authenticity ought to waft through the sixth sense. To throw the jargon around, to have a handy bit of lore in my pocket, I bought myself some books on the subject of fortune telling.

My Tarot cards, I learned, were for novices. "If we want the facts in detail," I told Edie, "I'll have to get a different deck."

Weiser's Occult Bookstore, the place for serious mystical paraphernalia, was no place for a girl like Edie. So when she asked, "What are we waiting for? Let's go get you new cards," I warned her, "No matter what the intentions are, should evil come, then evil will be returned threefold." That's a basic witchcraft rule of thumb but good advice regardless of your affiliations.

"They choose you. You don't choose them," the high priestess working the counter explained the method for selecting a deck of Tarot cards. She was weighted down with amulets, reeked of witch ointment, and had a pentacle tattooed on her chin. The high priestess was loony. But a loon who knew her trade. "As your hands pass over the cards, you'll detect an electrical sensation emanating from one deck. That is yours."

This ritual left Edie alone to wander. As I predicted, she zeroed in on the exact spot she should've stayed clear from. I got to her just as she was about to grab a book with a black cover and no title. I slapped her wrist. "Put that down."

Edie's arm suspended in mid-air. "What's the problem?"

"These books are trouble," I said.

"What sort of trouble? How should I know what to avoid if I don't know what it's about in the first place?"

"There are occasions," I told her, "when it's best to be ignorant. This is one of them."

"Nonsense." Edie'd never pick to be ignorant.

"Some things are beyond us," I said. "Take a close look at the people in here, Edie." She turned to check out the men with shaved heads wearing pajamas, a woman with six-inch fingernails painted onyx, a girl in a velvet cape with a boa constrictor wrapped around her neck. "It's a Halloween parade," I said. "Except it's the wrong season. This is what's beyond us. And frankly, I'd like to keep it that way."

Taking advantage of Edie's penchant for travel, I steered her to the section on Astral Projection. "Here. Busy yourself with a cost-free way to fly."

More than once, the Alister Crowley Tarot cards drew me close. The high priestess noted this with respect. Rumors circulated about those cards, that man, whispers of power run amok. But I chalked that up to silly superstition, paid for my cards, and went to get Edie where I'd left her. Only Edie'd vanished. To say she couldn't have simply disappeared might've made sense if we were in Barnes & Noble, but we were in Weiser's Occult Bookstore.

I found her outside sitting on the steps, reading. She held up her book to show me the cover, a man sleeping and a shadowy figure of the same man hovering above. "This is incredible, Monarose. You can go anywhere. First, you start out with little trips. Like to Trenton. But once you get good at it, you can hop the world like oceans were the backyard fence. I'm going to visit the Kremlin for starters." Edie put on her sad face. Some weeks before, Boris had been sent home to Moscow. He kissed Edie good-bye and said, "My work here is completed."

"No, it's not," she contradicted. "We don't have world peace, Boris. I don't see world peace. Do you see world peace?"

"There will never be world peace," Boris, that sly dog, said. "Not as long as there are women such as you. I understand this now. My country understands this now."

Even Edie couldn't work up a huff at such a kiss-off. The lies were sweeter than the man, and so Edie carried a torch for Boris, albeit dimly lit. "Won't he be tickled to find me at the Kremlin?" Edie put the book on Astral Projection in a red plastic bag. I noted it wasn't her only purchase. "What else did you buy?" I asked.

"More of the same," she told me. "I wish I'd learned of this sooner. When I think of all the money I spent on plane tickets, I could just spit."

I stood on the corner of 47th Street and 6th Avenue en route to a new job. I was in no hurry to get there to file papers, make coffee, when I collided with a boy I knew in college. He was a goofy boy. Edie detested him. In class, he offered his views like we were dying to hear

56

them. His views always wound up involving Plato. Plato must've been his hero. I didn't expect this boy to be pleased to see me. Yet he was positively beside himself. His attaché case banging at his knees, he told me he was in banking and just back from Liechtenstein. "Guess who I saw there?" he said.

"Plato," I guessed.

"No. I saw that friend of yours."

I didn't know anyone in Liechtenstein. I wasn't even sure where Liechtenstein was. "What friend?"

"That guy you palled around with. You and that awful girl."

"I still don't know who you mean. Describe him."

"Actually, he looks like that actor, Peter Finch."

"George. George is in Liechtenstein? What's he doing there?"

"I don't know," the goofy boy said. "He wouldn't tell me. He was very secretive."

Eager to get to the nearest pay phone, I said goodbye, nice to see you again. Fumbling through my purse for change, I called Edie and woke her up. "Remember that goofy guy in college who was hot for Plato?" I said. "I just ran into him."

"You call at nine in the morning to tell me that?"

"No. I called to tell you he's back from Liechtenstein and guess who he ran into there?"

"Where's Liechtenstein?" Edie asked.

"Damned if I know," I said, "but George does."

Through the phone I could feel her hackles rise. "George?" she said. "My George? Well, doesn't that explain everything." Edie told me she'd been having difficulty sleeping at night. Waking for no reason other than she sensed something. "A presence," she said.

"Like a ghost?"

"That's what I thought. But that's no ghost. That's George. He's astrally projecting himself here to harass me. He's got to know this mystical stuff. I'll bet he always knew it. I should've clopped him on both ears."

It wasn't in me to believe George was night-visiting at Edie's place. The way I expressed my doubt was, "Do you really think he'd come all the way from Liechtenstein simply to annoy you?"

"Yes, he would. He absolutely would." Edie was certain. "Now, what to do about it? Should I go find him, demand he stop and let me get a full night's sleep?"

"Where would you even begin to look? You don't even know where Liechtenstein is."

While conceding I had a point, it wasn't as if Liechtenstein couldn't be found. "We've got to work up a plan," Edie said. "Meet me at your place in an hour."

I glanced at my watch. "I'm on my way to a new job," I told her. "I'm already late."

"If you're already late, they're going to fire you anyway. Don't give them the pleasure. See you in an hour."

Edie walked in carrying a book, black cover, no title. "The answer is in here somewhere," she put the book down on my desk, "but I can't make sense of this stuff. You're smarter than me, Monarose. You'll decipher this book and help me win back George, won't you?"

"Since when are you interested in George again?" I asked.

"Well, maybe I'm not. But there must be thousands of tricks in here for us. We need to learn some new tricks," Edie said, "or we risk growing stale. You don't want us to grow stale, do you? Imagine us as stale, dried-out pieces of toast. Wouldn't that be awful? We mustn't let that happen."

A good portion of the black book dealt with raising the dead, not a skill we were keen on acquiring. The book also offered the key to serenity. Edie rolled her eyeballs at that. "What about love potions?" she asked.

The first love potion concerned winning the beloved away from a rival. I could've used that with my in-a-pinch married man. He'd punked out on me the moment he thought his wife was onto us. I read the spell which required a country road and menstrual blood laced with honey. Forget about that. He wasn't worth the effort. When he told me his wife was suspicious, and he said, "We'll have to work out another arrangement. I'm not sure I'll be able to see you as regularly for a while," I found, not only didn't I mind this, I was anxious to be done with him. "I think we ought to call it quits," I said and forced a single tear from my eye because I figured it was expected.

Mostly, the love spells in the black book were brews which called for plants now extinct, and it was assumed we could buy bat's claw at the local deli. The necessary herbs weren't tarragon or parsley, and alas, Cretan dittnay, fraxinella, deadly nightshade were not handy on the spice rack.

"What a pity we didn't live in an earlier time," Edie said. "We could've had boys falling at our feet like dominoes."

"In an earlier time," I mentioned, "if boys fell at our feet like dominoes, we'd be put to death. Burned at the stake."

"I could live with that," Edie said.

I turned to a brief chapter near the end of the book. "This might be the ticket for us," I said. "Mesmerism." Mesmerism wasn't the conventional brew in a cauldron. It didn't require locks of hair or poison mushrooms. No one had to eat toenail clippings while standing in a poppy field. While it did lack a certain flourish, I liked it. It was only staring, a fixed stare, mildly hypnotic. Staring deeply into the beloved's eyes, you transmit brain waves with messages attached. Messages about love, about how he'll do anything for you, suffer anguish, go into debt, write sonnets in your honor, scream like a hyena, all for want of you. By the time you blink, he's yours. All yours.

Edie was most eager to put a boy in a trance, stun him, and cart him off like a spider with a fly or Frankenstein with Elsa Lanchester.

What we needed was a guinea pig. Someone new. Someone we hadn't yet met. All the boys we knew had very decided notions about us, unlikely to be subject to change.

60

"Then we've got to go out stalking," Edie said.

I had an invitation to a cocktail party benefiting a community museum not in my neighborhood. I hadn't a clue as to how I'd gotten invited. "I hadn't planned on going but maybe I will," I said. "It'll be virgin territory. You can be my date."

Edie rubbed her hands together as if she were about to eat. "Some poor boy is going to love me more than I love him. How refreshing."

The day of the party, Edie and I practiced focusing on objects without looking off or blinking. "The lamp is in love with me," Edie declared. "So is the television."

I had a hunch the efficacy of mesmerizing would be enhanced if we looked pretty sensational. "What do you think we ought to wear?" I asked.

Edie wasn't sure, so I got out my copy of *Emily Post's Etiquette*, a 1934 edition. I held good etiquette to be timeless.

Emily Post was quite specific about proper cocktail party attire, only I didn't own to-the-elbow gloves or flouncy shin-length dresses like a Barbie doll wore.

Reading over my shoulder Edie pointed out, "It says here a fur wrap is appropriate. I've got my fur wrap." Edie's fur wrap was one of those things with the head and feet attached. She'd rescued it from a trash can, had it dry-cleaned, and named it Fluffy.

I found the passage we needed. "When in question, rely on something basic."

"Basic," Edie said, "as in basic black. You've got scads of dresses in black." She went to my closet and lifted out a few. Holding them up one at a time, she asked, "Did Emily Post win a Nobel Prize?"

Edie settled on a black crepe de chine with a lace back. I went with a jet beaded number which stopped three inches above my knees.

"You look sensational," Edie said. "Not everyone can pull off those beads." She draped Fluffy around her neck.

"Edie, that thing is a mess," I said. "It's lost its eyes."

"I know." Edie patted the balding head. "But Fluffy needs me. Someone threw it in the trash, Monarose. That was a terrible ordeal for Fluffy."

Standing at the mirror, I debated about jewelry. "Or should we go without? These dresses are kind of flashy."

"Diamonds," Edie decided. "Mounds of diamonds."

"Will rhinestones do?" I didn't own any diamonds.

"Rhinestones," Edie said, "are even better. I'm so partial to a fake."

We clipped on dangle earrings. Ropes of rhinestones sparkled around our necks. Edie added a wristful of bracelets. A dazzle of light refracted from us to the mirror and back. "Aren't we enchanting?" Edie said.

We should've worn tweeds. Straight from the office the others came in their pinstripe suits, dress-for-success ties, wing-tipped shoes. This held for the women, too. I leaned over to Edie and whispered, "If anyone asks, we were hired to pop out of a cake."

"Whatever do you mean, Monarose?"

"I mean," I said, "we're overdressed."

"Pshaw. There's no such thing as overdressed," Edie told me. "There's only standing out in a crowd. Now, let's find us a boy to bewitch."

While I was in the bathroom toying with my hair, Edie found Sam at the buffet table. She came to get me. "Quit fiddling and come along. I've got one cornered. He's kind of nice to look at, but you might not realize it because he's weak." Edie knew he was weak because he mumbled.

I followed Edie to the buffet table. "Sam," she introduced us, "this is Monarose. Don't mumble at her or she'll think you're weak." Sam said hello like he had a cracker in his mouth.

"See," Edie said as if he weren't there. "I told you. He mumbles."

I helped myself to a strawberry. Edie told Sam to stay put. "We'll be right back," she said. "Monarose and I have to discuss things."

Edie dragged me a couple of paces away. "What do you think?" she asked. "Isn't he perfect? Look at him. I tell him to stay put, and he doesn't dare even to breathe. Perfect, I tell you. Custom-made."

He might've been the perfect subject, but a party was no place to mesmerize. Too many distractions, and the lighting was far too bright. We needed to go someplace else.

"We're cutting out," Edie told Sam. "This party's a bore. Are you coming?"

Sam was there with a date. "She's around here some-where." He looked at the floor.

"So now you have two dates instead. You're not re-fusing us, are you?" Edie dared.

As a threesome, we walked along Third Avenue until we came to the Moonbeam Cafe. It was nearly empty, and the tables were candlelit. A flame was as trusty as a pocket watch.

Edie and I sat opposite Sam. He ordered a cappuccino. It left a line of steamed milk on his upper lip, which was not appealing. Gazing into his eyes was somewhat of a chore.

"So," he asked, "what do you girls do for a living?"

"Nothing," I said, and Edie told him we weren't girls. "We're women now. At least, I think we are. Last week we were definitely girls, but we've learned some new tricks since then."

Somehow, Sam twisted this and took it to mean we'd been to an encounter group or some such twaddle. He sang the praises of raising self-esteem, and Edie wanted to know if that were like raising the dead.

Sam got a little edgy. "I'm in computers. I design programs."

"We really don't care what you do," Edie said, so Sam asked where we lived. The next question on his list, which I suspected was drawn up ages ago and never revised, was if Edie and I saw anyone steadily.

"Speak up," Edie said. "It's an effort to listen to you."

"I was just wondering," Sam raised his voice, "if you two have steady boyfriends."

Edie threw up her hands in disgust. "This isn't working, Monarose. He doesn't know where to focus his attention."

"I know," I agreed, and I signaled the waitress for our check. Sam took out his wallet and asked, "Would you like to go for dinner?"

"Not tonight," Edie said. "But call us." She wrote her phone number, and mine, on a matchbook. Sam slipped it into his pocket. We waved him off and sat back down.

"He's utterly spineless," Edie marveled. "A joy to behold. He does what he's told, and we haven't even mesmerized him yet. Imagine the results we're going to get once he's under the spell. Our very own serf, Monarose."

Edie wanted me to go out with him first. The following night would be her turn to implement the four-step plan. "Mesmerize, seduce, toy with, and dump," she said.

"How much seduction do you have in mind?" I asked.

"Since when is seduction quantitative? Seduce him. Do the act with him."

I had no desire whatever to seduce Sam. "He leaves me cold," I said.

"That's because you are cold. You've got an ice cube for a heart."

"I am not cold," I grinned. "I just don't feel any sparks for Sam."

"That's because there aren't any. Sam wouldn't generate a spark if he stuck his finger in an electrical outlet.

65

But we have to sleep with him, Monarose. For science. For art. Besides, there's something pure about us having sex with the same boy. Don't you think there's something pure about it?"

Perhaps, if we liked Sam there'd be something pure about it, but as it was, sharing Sam was less significant than sharing cigarettes.

A wicked smile spread across Edie's face. "I'm so brilliant," she announced. "Let's go about it identically. Take him to the same place. Order the same dinner. Make the same conversation. You'll have to remember every word you say verbatim, so I can parrot it." Edie also thought we should wear the same style and color of underwear. "Let's go with a red bra and panties, black garter belt, black stockings."

"Why do we want to do all this? It's a lot of trouble to go to for a boy who ought to be effortless." Nothing in the black book mentioned double visions.

"Because," Edie explained, "when it's over, he'll have something to ponder. Let him know he's been trifled with by a higher source."

To tinker with him for the sport of it could be considered morally reprehensible. "This could be evil," I said, "and what then if evil comes?"

"Evil?" Edie made the word sound preposterous. "Why, Monarose, we're doing an act of kindness here."

"If you say so, Edie." I agreed to go along with this scheme of hers because it was something I'd never have thought of on my own, something I'd never have done if she hadn't suggested it. Therefore, if nothing else, it'd be a time worth remembering.

I finished my drink while staring into Sam's eyes. I ordered a refill without averting my gaze. Our appetizers came, and I didn't so much as blink as I ate my artichoke. I ran my chant, like it was a reel-to-reel tape, in my head. *You will fall madly in love with me. Hopelessly in love with me. You'll pine for me. Quit eating. Take up writing poetry. Bad poetry. You'll buy me presents. Expensive presents. You will fall madly in love with me. Hopelessly.* . . . Periodically, these thoughts were interrupted by a news bulletin: *I can't believe I let Edie talk me into this.*

"What are you thinking about?" Sam asked.

"I was thinking," I licked butter off two of my fingers, "how I want you to be in love with me."

Sam reached across the table and took my hands. His hands were moist. "This is wonderful," he said. "See, I'd been feeling really depressed lately. Until now. Now, I feel heavenly."

I hated when boys confided in me on a first date.

"I've never met anyone like you," Sam muttered. "Your eyes. Your eyes are . . ."

"Mesmerizing," I filled in the blank.

"Yes. That's it exactly. Mesmerizing."

"Let's get out of here," I said.

"But we didn't have our dinner," Sam noted.

"We don't need dinner," I told him.

In the taxi cab, Sam leaned in to kiss me.

"Don't," I pulled away. "I don't like public displays of affection." Actually, I adored public displays of affection. If I'd been attracted to Sam, I'd have gone at it with him in Barney's window. But I wasn't attracted to him, and Edie never said anything about having to kiss him. Mouth to mouth is far more intimate than pooch to pooch.

To bypass certain matters of course, I took off my dress while walking through my door, revealing my red-and-black underwear. Sam put his arms around me, and I hid my face in his shoulder. Let him kiss my neck, if he must, but I drew the line there.

"I think I'm falling in love with you," he mumbled into my hair.

"Good," I said.

"Are you falling in love with me?" he asked.

I broke away from him. "Take off your clothes," I said.

Sam did as he was told, but he was slow about things. "Hurry it up," I snapped.

"Yes, but part of me wants to linger over you." Sam mistakenly thought I was eager, aflame and aflutter with want for him.

"Forget the lingering," I said. "I haven't got all night." Because I didn't turn away fast enough, I caught the wounded look on his face.

Again Sam did as I instructed. He climbed on top of me and pumped madly. He made a noise, a yip, and it was over. I pushed him off of me.

"You're so beautiful," he whispered, as if we weren't alone.

"Go home, Sam," my voice boomed in comparison.

"Can't I stay the night? I want to wake up with yo
want to see you in the morning light."

"I look lousy in the morning light. Now go hom

"When can I see you again? How about tomorro

"Tomorrow you're going out with Edie," I reminded
him.

"I'll cancel," he said.

"Oh no, you won't." I was firm.

When I heard him go down one flight of stairs, I rang
up Edie. "Am I glad that's over with," I said.

"Has he gone?" she asked.

"Of course he's gone. Do you think I'd be calling you
with the dirt if he were still here?"

"I don't know," Edie said. "So tell me. Tell me all."

"A truly disgusting experience, Edie. Or else it was
just plain creepy. Well, you'll see for yourself."

"Do you really think that's necessary?" Edie asked. "As
long as we know this mesmerism works, what's the need
for further experimentation? Let's skip right to the good
stuff. Use it on boys we want. Forget about this Sam
person."

"That's not exactly sporting, Edie." I was miffed. "This
was your idea. You ought to go through with it, too."

"But to what end?" Edie asked. "Really, what's the
point?"

I didn't know what the point would've been, but I
reminded her of what she'd said about the purity of us
sharing the same boy. "Remember you said there was
something pure about that?"

"Perhaps I did say something along those lines," she

admitted. "But I can be wrong. We don't want to be pure. We want to avoid pure at all costs."

Astral Projection was not proving to be a quick and easy mode of transportation, as it was advertised. Edie still had to rely on public transportation, so we took the crosstown bus to a dollar-a-beer dive we were fond of when money was tight.

We sat at a corner table next to the jukebox, and Philip Estabrook pulled up a chair. "Hey, Mona," he said. Philip was chummy with my newest beau. Calvin and I had gone on a couple of double dates with Philip and his array of aspiring starlets. Philip favored dumb bunnies who nurtured the misconception that Philip could do wonders for their careers. He was a director in the theatre, but strictly East Village bush league. And at thirty-eight, with gray in his beard, it wasn't likely he'd be anything more.

Calvin was an actor, a good complement for me. He was pretty to look at and able to play enough parts to keep me amused. I liked him a lot, and when Edie asked, "Do you think you'll marry Calvin?" I said, "What? And spoil a good thing?" Calvin drank bourbon from a flask he kept in his jacket pocket, and we had experimental and amusing sex, sometimes involving costumes and props. Calvin was good fun.

"So who's your friend?" Philip was talking to me but gawking at Edie. He offered her his hand to shake. "Philip Estabrook," he said. "I'm in the theatre."

70

"What does that mean?" Edie asked. "Are you an usher?"

"Director." He aimed for cool but missed by a hair. "And I write a little."

I liked Philip well enough to spot him a beer, which he nursed until he got up to go. "Previous commitment," he said.

When he was gone, Edie sighed, "I love the way he smelled. Musky. Or musty."

Philip called me early the following morning. "I like your friend," he said.

"I like her too," I told him.

Philip wanted Edie's phone number. I was not inclined to give it to him. She was all wrong for Philip Estabrook. "She's very smart," I told him.

"I could tell." He claimed to find that intriguing.

"She's pretty headstrong, too. And temperamental." I was hedging.

"Come on, Mona. All I want is her phone number. I'm not going to hurt the girl. All I want to do is ask her out." Philip was mixed up. He thought it was Edie's welfare I was worried about.

"Don't say you weren't forewarned." I gave him what he was after. Breaking that connection, I called Edie and said, "Don't be mad at me," and I owned up to giving Philip her phone number.

"I'm not mad," she said. "He smelled nice. Does he always smell like that?"

71

———

Philip invited Edie out for dinner, but she didn't want to go. "Oh," she said. "You don't really want to go out, do you?" as if *out* were somewhere dreadful. "I'll make dinner," she offered. "At your place."

I sat in Edie's kitchen as she pored over a cookbook. "Why not pick up some Chinese food and be done with it?" I suggested.

Edie acted appalled and tried to convince me she'd be a whiz in his kitchen. "All I ever wanted to be was a housewife," she declared. "I'll make a lovely housewife."

I reached under the chair and lifted up a dustball the size of a cantaloupe. "Yeah. You'll be real lovely at it. And let us not forget that dessert you always make."

"Pudding-In-A-Cloud." She beamed.

Pudding-In-A-Cloud was an Oliver Twistian nightmare. Canned chocolate pudding swirled with imitation whipped cream. Real cream doesn't marbleize and set in place. This dessert was a cornucopia, churning and multiplying in the bowl. "Edie," I said, "girls who really want to be housewives don't whip up that sort of item."

"They don't?"

"You've nothing to offer a husband," I said. "You make a great mistress but, from any angle, you'd be a terrible wife."

"I can try, can't I?"

"Yes, you can try." I was confident she didn't have a clue as to where to begin.

Edie's date with Philip ended on an upbeat note. She was moving into his building. Not into his apartment but into the one directly below it.

Philip didn't discover Edie's lack of culinary ability because, instead of eating, they spent the evening rolling around on the floor. "Literally on the floor," Edie told me. "I've got rug burns in places you wouldn't believe. Anyway, I mentioned how the people below him must be getting an earful. That's when he said the apartment was vacant."

The rent was half what she was paying. It had a fireplace and the tub was in the kitchen. "Bathing in the kitchen is erotic, don't you think? So I called the landlord first thing this morning. I'm on my way to sign the lease now."

"What about having Philip directly overhead? Are you going to like that?"

"Like it? He's a pound on the ceiling away. One date and we're practically living together. That's progress."

Helping Edie move wasn't even a half day's work. All she owned was a bed, a desk, two folding chairs, and a kitchen table. Her stereo, typewriter, books, and records went into cartons. Dishes, pots, and pans were left behind. In a pillowcase she put the blue ceramic Egyptian cat I'd bought her one birthday, an 8 × 10 blow-up of Check Point Charley framed, her map of the world, and her clocks. Edie had seven or eight clocks, none set for the right time. Because she didn't believe in Daylight Savings, the clocks were off half the year regardless. Those needing to be wound, never were. One was missing the big hand. Another, a tribute to her old flame Boris, ran on Moscow time.

While we waited for the moving van, Edie said, "You didn't tell me Philip is married."

"Was married," I corrected.

"He still is married," Edie informed me. "He never got divorced. He's been separated for thirteen years. His wife lives in Chicago. They stay married because she's got a health insurance plan that covers him. I could get one of those. If I set my mind to it, I could get a health insurance plan for me and my husband, couldn't I? And we could cut a hole in the ceiling and put in a staircase. I've always wanted a duplex."

"Instead of a staircase, why not a pole? Like they have in firehouses. You could shimmy up and down."

Edie gave a snort and stamped her feet. "I'm serious. This is perfect. You and Calvin and me and Philip. We could be like the Flintstones and the Rubbles, best friends who go bowling together. I'm perfect for him. Inspirational. He can write plays about me. Give me immortality."

We got Edie moved and set up in her new apartment as if she were one step ahead of the law. My apartment, with seven busy years crammed into one room, resembled an overstuffed brocade chair bursting from too much filling. "It would take me months to move," I thought out loud.

"Oh no, Monarose." Edie gasped. "Don't even think about moving. You can't. You have to stay put. Your apartment is a constant. We need the stability."

From the deli downstairs, we bought four cups of coffee and set them on Edie's table. "This move was a good idea, wasn't it?" she asked.

"Sure. Think of what you'll be saving on rent."

"Read the Tarot," Edie requested. "Let's find out if the cards approve this move."

It was a little late for that, but I got my Tarot cards from my purse. Edie shuffled them. I cut the deck, left to right, into three piles. Making seven columns, I turned over twenty-one cards.

As well as I could read the symbols of cups and wands, Edie could read me. "What's wrong?" she asked. "Am I going to die?"

"You're not going to die, Edie."

Most of the cards were the same ones that popped up regularly for Edie. Adventure. Travel. Greed. The card that cautions against bad temper. "What's this one about?" Edie put her finger on one she'd never seen before. It was the 17th Trump, a castle burning, havoc reigning.

It meant trouble. Ugly times ahead. Things falling apart, going up in smoke. To tell this to Edie would ruin her day. And mine. "Oh, that one. That one means you've just moved. You've left a place behind. You've gone on to a new place. A better place. The old place is in shambles."

"Does it say anything else? Anything about the boy upstairs? That's got a nice ring to it. The boy upstairs. Doesn't that have a nice ring to it?"

CRIME AND PUNISHMENT

4

Philip Estabrook seemed promising. Often we went out as a foursome, so I got to watch as Edie made him laugh. "You're whack-o," he'd say. He toted her to his theatre gatherings. He cooked her dinner. He saw to it she was not hungry. He gave her keys to his apartment, a token Edie put in the same category as an engagement ring.

Philip genuinely liked Edie, although she wasn't at all what he was used to. And alas, his idea of change had to do with four quarters to a dollar. He was accustomed to girls who said little but wiggled a lot. Edie's challenges began to rattle him. "You're so contrary. Always disagreeing with me. Why do you argue so much?" he asked her. "And why do you throw things? And why do you ask me to get married every twenty minutes?" Philip asked Edie to give back his keys and said, "Let's be friends."

"Why would I want to be friends with you?" Edie said. "The only thing I ever liked about you was your smell."

"You know, you're not right," Philip said.

As if dumping Edie weren't criminal enough, Philip had the gall to bounce back into circulation fast. He wasted not one Friday night before dating with a frenzy, filling up on starlets like a swimmer coming up for air.

Edie watched through her peephole as this parade of girls went up the stairs. "Actress types eating my shrimp in garlic butter, drinking my beer. What am I going to do about this?" She wasn't really asking me. Rather, to herself she said, "I want satisfaction."

When Edie was a child, she once placed a boy's head in a vise. "I was going to crush his skull," she told me. "Only my grandmother came rushing into the toolshed to investigate what all the hollering was about."

Later that day, Edie's mother took her to Dairy Queen for a strawberry sundae. Edie never got punished, not for anything, because her mother had to compensate for her father. Frequently, Edie's father got married to well-to-do widows and truck-stop waitresses. Edie needed no compensation for such a father but was clever enough to make out very well with the setup. "After all," she said, "who could blame poor little me for any misdeed when I had a cad for a father and so many wicked stepmothers? It's the children who suffer most," Edie said with glee.

I experienced envy over her family arrangement. My family was so stable, we were inert. Mine was a dreary upbringing compared to Edie's. No wonder I didn't have her panache. My parents never even *talked* divorce.

Not that revenge didn't have a place in the scheme of things, and Philip did deserve it, but I thought it wiser to allow circumstances to do my dirty work. People get what they deserve in the end.

"That could take weeks," Edie argued. "Better to make the bastard bleed now. Allowing the guilty to get off scot-free is un-American, Monarose. Why do you think we have courts and judges and juries? To hang the guilty," she pronounced. "Crime must not go unpunished."

Edie dumped the contents from a brown paper bag onto my bed. Tubes and wires tumbled out in a jumble.

I picked up a red wire, twirled it between my fingers. "What possessed you to take apart a radio?" If Edie'd developed a scientific bent, I'd have expected her to study brain folds, scouting for long-kept secrets, or to dissect the human heart and examine it for faults.

"It's not exactly a radio," Edie told me. "It's parts. For a bug. You can't buy a whole one. They're not for sale unless you've got your CIA credentials handy. I got escorted from three electronic shops before I found a nice man willing to help me. Then he invited me to lunch, but he withdrew the offer when I asked if he really wanted to date a girl who was about to bug her ex-boyfriend's apartment."

"Edie, you're not going to do that."

"I most certainly am." Edie rubbed her hands together. "I'm going to get such dirt on him, learn all there is to know, find out what these starlets have that I don't have."

"They don't have anything you don't have."

"They must have something," Edie disagreed. "They're with him and I'm not."

Morally speaking, it's okay to read your boyfriend's mail provided it's already been opened. Breaking the seal isn't nice. Postcards are always fair game. Snooping in a lover's apartment is permissible, but snooping in a friend's is not. I wouldn't balk at making a few phone calls to check character and credit references, "but," I said, "bugging is a lousy thing to do."

"Haven't you any sympathy for me?" Edie asked. "Where's your compassion? It's easy for you to be all high and mighty. You've never suffered flat-out rejection. You don't know what it's like to have a boy tire of you."

"Philip didn't tire *of* you, Edie. He tired *from* you." Not that I cared one whit about Philip's civil rights. It was Edie's need for extremes, the unrestrained killing of the dead, that left me uneasy. "Some things are sacred," I said.

"That's true, Monarose. Love is sacred. He spat on it, and now he'll pay the price."

Days passed and there was no more talk of wiretapping, bugging devices, or covert operations until one Sunday night when Edie called me. "You've got to come over," she said. "Right away."

On her kitchen table was a tape recorder. Edie motioned for me to sit down, relax. She pressed the *Play* button.

Philip's voice came through the speaker: *You do things to me. I think about you. I think about licking you. Starting with your toes. I want to suck your toes.*

Giggle, giggle. Titter. Giggle. Tee-hee.

"That's Tanya," Edie said. "Or that's what she calls herself. Probably a stage name."

We listened to Philip tell Tanya she was sleek like a leopard. Her muscle tone excited him.

"Do you believe this?" Edie asked. "What crummy dialogue."

"Did he talk to you like that?"

"I doubt it. I'd never have allowed it," Edie said.

Tanya, apparently, had no such objections. *You're a real wild man.*

"The leopard and the wild man. Like a Tarzan movie," I noted.

Edie put her finger to her lips. "This is the best part."

Slurping noises were followed by moans. Zippers unzipped. Clothing rustled. *Oh, Tanya.* Bedsprings creaked. *Oh, Philip. Oh, God.* Sex on a tape recorder sounded like wine tasting. Or the noise a dog makes after you feed it peanut butter.

"Didn't that little bug pick up plenty?" Edie was tickled with her success.

I asked how she managed to plant the microphone.

80

As amusing as this was, I didn't want her to be guilty of breaking and entering, too.

"I've got keys," she told me.

"I thought he asked for them back."

"He did. And I gave them to him. But I had copies made first. An even dozen. You want a set?"

This recording session, while potentially embarrassing for Philip, wasn't the stuff of blackmail. He couldn't be ruined by this. "He won't pay ransom," I said.

Edie knew that. "But it sure can put a kink in a good time." She went to her fireplace and picked up a blue wire. "See this? This baby runs up the chute to Philip's fireplace. From there, it's hooked to his stereo speakers. All we do now is attach the microphone to this end and play our tape."

"No doubt he'll blush at hearing this again, but why all this trouble just to let him know he's been spied on?"

"Think big, Monarose. He's got a girl up there now. And this girl is not Tanya."

Edie hooked up the equipment and shut off the lights. "Be very quiet," she instructed. "Otherwise he'll pick up our voices, too." Edie rewound the tape and turned the volume up full blast.

The tape played out to the end before we got any response. "Maybe I ought to run it again," Edie whispered just as we heard Philip charge down the stairs. Edie and I sat as still as a pair of cement library lions.

"Edie!" Philip pounded at her door. "Open up. I know you're in there. Open this fucking door."

When he gave up and went away, we took our hands

from our mouths. After a fine laugh, I told Edie I was very glad I was her friend. "I'd never want to be on your bad side."

"But you'd never cross me, Monarose."

Edie's yen for revenge should've been satisfied with the bugging session, but there was too much temptation in Philip's proximity to stop her.

Whenever Edie saw Philip go out, she let herself in his apartment. There she made little messes. Dumping an ashtray on the floor. Breaking a dish. Clogging the toilet with his address book. One afternoon, overcome with a desire to smell him again, she decided to confiscate his favorite shirt.

"Go figure it." She talked to me from inside his closet. "I did love his smell. Got it." She stepped out clutching a denim shirt. "Do you want anything?" Edie invited me to poke around Philip's things. "Help yourself," she said as if she were holding out a tray of canapes.

I took a blue-and-green paisley Nehru jacket. "Look at this. It's an antique."

"There is something very sorry about a man who can hold on to a jacket for twenty-some-odd years but can't keep a girl more than a few weeks."

We ran into Philip outside by the deli. We would've kept walking had he not grabbed Edie by the sleeve. "Someone's been in my apartment," he said. "Wrecking the place. Taking my things. Drinking my beer."

"Why, you sound just like Papa Bear," Edie smirked.

"From that story with the blonde-headed girl. Doesn't he 1sound just like Papa Bear, Monarose?"

I bobbed my head yes.

"Maybe you've got poltergeists," Edie suggested. "If I were you, I'd move. Your place is haunted."

"Give me back my keys," Philip held out his hand. "I know you've got a set. I want them."

Edie took two keys hooked to a paper clip from her back pocket. She dangled them out before letting them drop to the ground. Philip picked up his keys without comment.

"The trouble with him," Edie said to me, "is he doesn't think big."

The sounds, and sight, of an ax hacking apart her door woke Edie from a deep sleep. She'd had dreams of this nature before. Thinking little of it, she rolled over.

"Get up." The man with the ax shook her.

"Are you for real?" Edie thought her dreams were taking a new twist, crossing lines.

"Yes, I'm for real. Now get up." The fireman told Edie to vacate the premises immediately.

Wrapping herself in her blanket, she followed the fireman into the hallway and down the stairs. "It was like hell, an inferno," she described. "The road under the volcano. Thick with black smoke. A beam broke and fell in our path. The fire cackled like the devil's laugh."

Huddled around the fire trucks were the other tenants. Edie'd been the last one out. Philip rested against one of the red engines, drinking coffee from a Styrofoam cup.

Gathering her blanket around her like a sarong, Edie marched up to him and demanded, "How long have you been out here?"

"A while," he said.

"Exactly how long is a while?"

Philip shrugged. "I don't know. Before the firemen got here. I was the one who called them."

"Why didn't you knock on my door on your way down?" Edie wanted to know.

Philip backed away a couple of steps. "How was I supposed to know you were even home? What difference does it make now? It's not like anything happened to you."

"You would've let me burn," Edie said. "I had sex with you. Repeatedly. But you would've let me burn. I loved you, and you would've let me sizzle, burn, and char to a crisp."

As if Venetian blinds were opening to let in the day, slats of sunlight broke through the periwinkle sky. The fire was out. The building was declared safe.

Edie's place was wet, and it smelled bad, but there wasn't much damage. I helped her clean up. Picking up the carpet, a remnant meant to pass as a kilim, I said, "This is waterlogged, Edie. There's no saving it."

"He would've let me burn," she said for the umpteenth time. "That leaves an impression. I was the last one out. In a fire. He would've let me burn."

———

A cold spell hit. The air bit and stung and was hell on the complexion. Edie and I holed up in our respective apartments and logged in lots of telephone time. Outside, the wind sliced sharply and cried as if the city were possessed by lost souls.

Late into such a night, there was a knock on my door. "Don't answer it," Calvin nibbled at my earlobe.

I pushed him off me and got out of bed. Slipping on a robe, I went to the door and looked through the peephole. There was Edie standing in the hallway shivering like an orphan. I let her in, and she said, "I have to stay here. I brought provisions." Edie unloaded a grocery sack of coffee, beer, cigarettes, and crackers. She popped open a Beck's and then noticed Calvin in my bed. "What's he doing here?" she asked.

"What do you think I'm doing here?" Calvin said.

"He has to leave," Edie said to me. "Now. I have to talk to you, Monarose. Alone. Now," she emphasized.

"No way." Calvin pulled the blankets around himself tightly. "I'm not going anyplace."

The window panes rattled with a gust of wind, and I said, "Come on, Calvin. Edie needs to talk to me."

"If you put me out," Calvin warned, "I'll never come back. I swear, Mona. That's it with us."

"Calvin, leave," Edie said.

Calvin looked at me, and I nodded. "You better go," I told him.

"It's over, then. You get that?" he asked me.

"Yes. I understand."

Calvin dressed in a rush and stormed out the door.

Edie was quiet for a moment, and then she said, "If anyone calls looking for me, tell them I'm in Miami where any sane person would be on a night like this."

"Who's looking for you?"

"Philip."

"Philip? Weren't we done with Philip? Why's he looking for you now?"

"Because I just broke his windows. With a hammer," she added. "I wanted him to feel like I did. Like dry ice."

Edie, cold and lonely, climbed out onto her fire escape, a hammer tucked in her waistband. She went up one flight and peeked through the window. Philip and some babe were snuggled under a blanket. Edie held the hammer and bashed the glass. Quickly sidestepping to the living room windows, she shattered those, too. "It must be so freezing in there. And pray tell, however will he get a repairman at this time of night?"

We smoked a cigarette each, and Edie finished her beer. When the telephone rang, I looked at her and asked, "Should I answer it?"

"Definitely," Edie said. "Who else will tell him I'm in Florida?"

I feigned grogginess, but Philip wasn't at all concerned that he might've woken me. "Where is she?" he said.

"Where is who?"

"You know damn well who. That crazy bitch broke my windows. Put her on the phone, or I'll call the cops and have her arrested."

"I don't know what you're ranting about," I said. "I was sleeping. You woke me."

"Put Edie on the phone," Philip repeated.

"Edie's in Florida with all the other sane people. You know how she likes to fly places."

"Yeah," Philip said. "I know. She flew up the fire escape and broke my windows."

"What makes you think it was Edie? It could've been anyone." That was a pretty absurd thing for me to say, and Philip let me know so. "Honest," I swore. "She's in Florida."

"You shouldn't cover for her." Philip's voice calmed. "She wouldn't do the same for you."

"We don't know that," I said. Then I recommended Philip patch the windows with cardboard. "Until you can get them fixed. Cardboard works better than a blanket."

I hung up the phone and told Edie, "He's furious. He threatened to call the police. You don't want to get arrested. Not even for a crime of passion. Maybe going away for a few days isn't such a bad idea."

"Hide out until the heat dies down," she laughed as the cold winds howled wickedly, too. "Oh." She had an afterthought. "I hope you don't feel bad about Calvin. You were too good for him, you know. Granted, he's pretty but really only in a soap-opera style. And face it, Monarose. He didn't have much to say."

"I know," I agreed. "But that was sort of what I liked about him."

Instead of heading south to Florida, Edie boarded a Lufthansa DC-10 bound for Vienna, probably the only spot on the map colder than New York that week.

After three days of sacher tortes, sausages, decayed splendor, and old ladies walking dachshunds, Edie had her fill of Vienna. She returned with a front of warmer air.

It wasn't yet spring. There was no tangible evidence of rebirth, no daffodils or wide-mouthed baby birds, yet it seemed a fresh start. "It's getting better, Monarose," Edie said. "From here on in, it's going to be something else."

JUST GIRLS

5

At one of the international banks at Rockefeller Center, Edie slid a handful of Austrian coins to the teller.

"I'm sorry," the teller said. "We accept paper money only. Next," she called.

Edie refused to budge. "This is good money. There's nothing wrong with this money."

"Bank rules," the teller said. "Paper money only. Perhaps if you go to—"

"Perhaps you can go to—" Edie didn't get a chance to complete her thought either. A man intervened.

"A handsome, middle-aged man," Edie told me. "He was dressed like a banker, but he had the cutest accent.

Just like Colonel Klink's. And he asked, 'Vut is the problem here?' Vut? Isn't that cute?"

Out of his own pocket, he exchanged the money for Edie. "He gave me a much better rate than the bank would've. His name is Werner." Edie scrunched up her nose. Werner was not a name easily called out in the heat of passion.

Edie renamed him "my Kraut," because she favored an ethnic slur whenever she could get away with one. And this particular slur brought home the fact that, NATO be damned, the Germans are, and always will be, the enemy.

The Kraut and Edie lunched together often. Lunch was chocolates nibbled on between courses of what Edie claimed was fantastic sex. "Really fantastic," she said. "I'm not making it up this time. I'm actually having orgasms."

"You mean you weren't having orgasms before? Why would you bother having sex if you weren't having orgasms?"

Edie shrugged. "Optimism, maybe. And with Philip I did sometimes. But not like this. Not always and in triplicate."

Before returning to the bank, Werner peeled off some twenties from his billfold and said, "You und Mona vill have a good dinner," like he was giving an order.

"You know," Edie pocketed the money, "I'm crazy about you."

Werner thought *crazy about you* was an expression Edie invented. "Yes," he said. "Crazy about. Zat explains everysing."

"Let's be really crazy about each other." Edie covered him with kisses. "Let's run off together."

"Vere to?" he asked.

"Verever you want," Edie promised him. "We could live in Palm Springs. We could drive a Mercedes. Or a Volkswagen. We could live in a house mit pool and Japanese garden."

"Und how long before you vouldn't vant me anymore?"

"I'll always want you." Edie was very sincere. "You're my Kraut. I'll want you forever."

"Und how long," Werner asked, "is forever in America?"

Edie decided that was the most profound question ever raised. For weeks, she put it to everyone with whom she spoke. "Tell me," she asked, "how long is forever in America?"

Some weeks, Edie didn't see her Kraut for four or five days at a clip. He took a lot of business trips. Other weeks, she might not see him for a few days running if he weren't able to sneak away from Ingrid. Ingrid was the woman he'd been living with for seventeen years.

"He couldn't love her," Edie reasoned. "After seventeen years, if you love someone, you marry them. You make a commitment." Nonetheless, Edie was hell-bent on sizing up her competition. "I need to see her. Just a peek."

We staked out Werner's apartment building. Under

the fish eye of the doorman, we moseyed by again and again, straining our ears for a German accent. "You're sure this is the right address?" I asked.

"Positive." Edie'd gone through Werner's wallet. "All papers lead here. Maybe Ingrid doesn't do anything except stay home, vatch game shows, und bake strudel."

We were about to call it quits, head back downtown, when the gutteral sounds of German wafted our way. Ingrid, it had to be Ingrid, was reprimanding the doorman. "Vere ver you last night? You ver away from your post."

Ingrid was small in stature, although she seemed neither delicate nor childlike the way small women often do. Her voice and manner added bulk to her frame, leaving the impression she was squat. She was wearing a fox fur coat. Ingrid did not cut a particularly attractive figure.

"And I thought those fox fur coats made everyone look glamorous," Edie said. "Maybe that's not her."

"Who else could it be?" I asked.

"Their maid?"

"In a fox fur coat? Giving the doorman grief? If you could bake a strudel, Edie, he'd be yours forever."

Plotting, scheming, lounging, and lollygagging suited Edie the way the countryside suits English girls. Her cheeks took on a healthy blush. She was animated, giggly, and a pound or two heavier. "I'm just wasting away from love," she said.

With a generosity she could then easily afford, Edie

wanted me to be in love, too. "I want you to pine along with me, Monarose. Isn't there anyone for you to love today?"

There was someone. A possibility. He lived, or worked, near me. Each day, when I was at my mailbox, he walked by. After a while, we acknowledged each other with a nod. Then a smile. We'd recently worked our way up to hello. "I like his face. It has character. He's got wrinkles," I told Edie. "But I don't know a thing about him, except I'd estimate he's twice my age."

"Older men are divine," Edie said. "They understand women. How to please us. Plus, they are grateful. My Kraut's got years on me. Almost twenty of them. Of course, no amount of time can compensate for his being German. Loving him is practically treason. Oh, be in love, Monarose. It's more fun when we're both in love. Do it for me."

Oh, the joy we suffered, intoxicating little pains. Daily, we pressed at the bruises to keep them blue, purple, and pretty.

Once I had a boyfriend who said to me, "Sometimes, I think if you had to choose between Edie and me, you'd pick Edie." I didn't answer him, and he went on, "It makes me feel like we don't have a future together." He was right about that, too.

"I'm thinking about converting," Edie said as she chomped into an apple.

"Converting to what?"

93

"Jewish. I could pass. I look more Jewish than you do. My Kraut thought I was Jewish. He was disappointed when I said I wasn't. I should've lied. I think he wants a Jewess." Edie'd worried that, on the basis of this Jewish issue, Werner might decide to love me instead of her. "So when he asked if you were Jewish, I said no. I said you were Spanish. Your people were from Barcelona."

My people were not from Barcelona, but nor was I anyone's idea of a Jewess, either. To say I was assimilated was to understate the watering down of my ethnicity. I was raised on shrimp salad sandwiches, the crust cut away. "I'm barely Jewish," I said to Edie.

"Since when did a German care about a qualifier when it came to a Jew? *Barely* would've landed you in the same place as *devoutly.* I really think my Kraut wants me to become Jewish."

"No rabbi would convert you, Edie. You have to give a reason for conversion. And the desire to be forbidden fruit to tempt a German lover isn't a reason the rabbi wants to hear."

"Why not?" Edie asked. "It's a good reason. The best reason."

"Look at that," Edie said to me. "Happiness. Right smack in front of us where we can kick it in the face."

We were on our way to Brooklyn. We'd come to prefer going to Brooklyn to going abroad. Plenty of people boast of having been to London, but how many of them get to

94

see Seagate or Canarsie? When asked about my travels, I sometimes forgot I'd been to Venice, but I always remembered Bensonhurst, where the front yards featured cement Jesuses and Marys housed in glass cases.

In Europe, Edie and I never did much more than hang around cafés. But in Brooklyn, we explored side streets, alleyways, courtyards. We brought our cameras. We took in the sights.

The Arab district along Atlantic Avenue isn't much of a district. Just some restaurants, a pita bread bakery downstairs in a dank celler which could've been a slave market, and some spice shops. It was the spice shops that lured us there. We needed to refill our supply of kohl.

Although all the spice shops stocked kohl, we had a favorite. A very old guy worked the counter. His hair was white, his teeth gold. His suit was blue and dated. He was serious about spice.

This was our fourth visit to his shop in as many years. Edie believed the old man remembered us well, despite evidence to the contrary. She greeted the man as if they'd grown up together. "It's been a long time," she said. "How have you been?"

He said nothing. Edie turned to me and explained, "It's a game he plays with me, to keep the air of mystery going." Then she told him, "We're here for our kohl."

"Kohl? Why do you wish for kohl? Kohl is for Arab women."

"You're a stitch," Edie laughed. "Each time I come here, we have this conversation. Go on, now. I'm with

95

you." She showed him her profile and asked, "Don't I look like an Arab woman? Aren't I the spitting image of an Egyptian queen?"

The old man was a wizard when it came to concealing his thoughts. Deadpan, except for his gold teeth flashing at her, he considered Edie again. "Yes," he said. "Now that I look twice, you do."

With our kohl tucked in our pocketbooks, Edie and I waved good-bye to the old man. "It's a good thing we go around together," Edie said to me. "He'd never sell you the kohl if you weren't with me."

I smiled at Edie much the way the old man did. "Yes, my friend," I said. "I believe that is so."

Edie stopped at the window of a store selling records, tape cassettes, and outfits for belly dancers. The outfit on display was a knockout. Purple sequined bra, chiffon pants the color of a desert sky at night. I picked up fast on what Edie was thinking and said, "Forget about it."

We'd long ago accepted my ability to second-guess her. Edie was firm it was because I had the gift. I figured it came from knowing her as well as I did. Sometimes I'd spook her a little by mouthing her response, word for word, a split second ahead of her.

"But Monarose," she argued, "the Kraut would love me in that outfit."

"No, he wouldn't," I said. "It's a mixed metaphor."

"If I put on that costume, I could get him to run off with me to Baghdad."

"Baghdad is in Iraq, Edie. No one can run off to Iraq. Not international bankers. Not even you. Forget the costume. It's more than we could afford." Affordability had to do with more than money. If Edie bought the belly dancer's outfit, she'd only want it for the kick of owning it, trying it on. Then, she'd unload it on me. Once I had it, I'd take up belly dancing and work bachelor parties.

Edie stood firm on the sidewalk until I got her to admit the outfit wasn't anything more than a whim. "You're right," she said finally. "How is it you're always right?"

At the Moroccan Star, the waiter delivered our shish kebabs. Edie sliced a piece of meat in two, and stabbed one half with her fork. "I need to be sure the Kraut loves me. How am I going to get him to prove it?" Edie wasn't going to rest until Werner left Ingrid, vacated his uptown apartment, quit his job—all for love of Edie. She wanted him to give up strudel, forget about currency exchange rates and ski weekends. Still, she was after proof she could hold in her hand.

"When he tells you he loves you, why don't you simply believe him?" I asked.

"Get real, Monarose," Edie said. "Tell me, how many times have you professed love when you didn't mean it? It's natural to lie about such things."

Edie couldn't have really wanted a full-time German underfoot. A German in the house is nowhere near as exciting as having one on the sly. "Look at it this way," I said. "If sex is like a drink of water, doesn't it taste more like champagne if a drought's on? If all you have to do is go to the kitchen and turn on the tap, water tastes merely like water. And picture this, Edie. A German will insist on a clean house, sterile. You'll have to serve Werner breakfast each morning on clean plates while he folds his *Times* into precise quarters."

"Breakfast?" Edie made a face. "Who eats breakfast?"

"Don't mess with perfection," I told her. "You've got the ideal setup going. Leave it alone."

"This sure is a nice day we're having, isn't it, Monarose?"

"Yes. Now eat your shish kebab. It's getting cold."

Edie ate a bite and asked, "Are we content?"

I recoiled at the word. "Please, Edie. Cows are content. Content is a word reserved for cows chewing their cud."

"Monarose? What is cud, anyway?"

"Not something we'd ever chew," I said.

"I didn't think so." Then Edie asked, "We are happy girls though, aren't we?"

98

THE ONLY TRUTH I KNEW

6

Werner was hurrying from Edie's building as I was going in. He nodded to me, a curt nod, as if he and I were undercover agents who shouldn't really be acknowledging each other.

Edie's door was ajar. I pushed it open and found Edie sitting yoga-style on her bed, surrounded by shards of broken ashtrays, coffee cups in pieces. Books were off the shelves, covers torn away, pages pulled out by the roots. I picked up a piece of a record album, Blondie's *Heart of Glass*, and dropped it in the trash can.

I'd seen a house look this way once. On the news. A tornado had cut a path through a living room in Indiana. "What happened here?" I asked.

Werner was being transferred home to Frankfurt. He was ordered to settle his affairs here and get packing.

"That could be swank," I said. "A cross-continental romance."

"I don't want a cross-continental romance." Her jaw set. "I want him here. A cab ride away."

It didn't take much for Edie to pop off. A blemish. A less than perfect haircut. A run in a stocking. A lover being transferred to Frankfurt. It was hard to know which really cut to the bone. Was a chipped nail more painful than a broken zipper? Did a lost earring cause more grief than a lost boyfriend? I could never tell. All I knew was that I was expected to fix it, whatever it was. "There are other boys," I said.

"Oh, I know that. Boys who disappear with no forwarding addresses. Boys who never had addresses to begin with. Boys who run away from me. And boys who would let me burn while the building went up in flames. I want a boy who sticks by me. Why can't I have that, Monarose?"

At the deli downstairs, in the aisle between cat food and canned soups, Edie collided with a boy who lived on her block. "I'd seen him around before," she told me, "but didn't notice him because I was busy with someone else. You want to hear something sweet?" she asked.

"Probably not."

"He called me Snow White. I was wearing that white

100

skirt, the full one. And a ratty old white sweatshirt. I must've looked frightful, but he said, 'Hey, Snow White, you want to pass me a can of those baked beans?' Isn't that darling?"

"Precious," I said.

"I could like this boy, Monarose. I could love him. I could love that he lives on my block. I could love a boy who stays put. So," she asked, "should I write him a note declaring my intentions? I can slip it in his mailbox. I know where he lives. Or is that too brash?"

To act coy was an utter waste of time. "Write the note," I said. "What have you got to lose?"

Edie phoned me the next morning with a question. "Can a person improve in bed once they're over twenty-one?"

"You mean yourself?"

"No, I mean him."

"Oh. I don't know. Hold on, I'll ask Ross." I posed Edie's question to the man in my bed, the one with the wrinkles, whom I met at my mailbox. He was a musician and, indeed, twice my age.

"I should hope so," Ross said, and I relayed that to Edie.

"Oh, good. I had such a wonderful time last night," she said, although those dots didn't connect. "I left the note like you told me to. He called me the minute he got it and came over. Gerald is fascinating. He's an entre-preneur."

Entrepreneur was a profession I couldn't get a handle on. I'd assumed it was a polite way of saying drug dealer, the way *consultant* and *escort* are euphemisms, too.

"Oh, no," Edie said. "Gerald is very opposed to drugs."

"Is he a fanatic?" I asked.

"Sort of. But not in a weird way. He's very forceful. Intense. He's got strong ideas. He's very unique. Honestly, he's like a genius."

It was nice to think you could find a genius next to the rack of Moon Pies at the deli downstairs.

After Edie and I hung up, Ross wanted to know, "What was that all about?"

"Edie's got a new squeeze," I told him.

"Edie." He rolled his eyes.

"I thought you liked her."

"I do like her," he said. "But it's all kind of childish, telling each other every little thing. Best friend silliness."

"If we were sisters, instead of friends, would you think we were silly?"

Ross conceded he would not, that if we were sisters such intimacy would seem natural. Then he said, "Maybe I don't like her. She is kind of a headache, you know."

"You couldn't like me but not like Edie," I said. "It's not possible. We're a team. A duo. Besides," I confessed, "if it weren't for her, I'd be a garden variety girl. Ordinary."

"You give her far too much credit," Ross said. "You're quite remarkable in your own right." He kissed the palm of my hand, and it registered there were some things no one but Edie and I would ever really appreciate.

"Guess what?" Edie asked, after three days of being impossible to reach.

My patience for guessing games was negligible. "I don't want to guess. I hate guessing."

"I'm getting married." Edie said this breathlessly, rehearsed.

"To someone in particular?" I asked.

"To Gerald. Who did you think?"

"I don't know. I haven't spoken to you in days. It could be anyone."

"We're going to get married as soon as possible. Aren't you excited?"

"I'm delirious." I said. Getting engaged was fun for twenty-four hours. After that, engagements were tedious. Edie would grow tired of it. But for that day, it was an excuse to drink champagne.

It was my suggestion we get Champale, that pink crap which was equally as ridiculous as Edie's plan to marry and be a wife.

"No. Real champagne," Edie said, and she came over with a bottle of Moët.

The next night we should've had champagne again. To toast Edie's unengagement. We should've clinked glasses and said, "Here's to what's-his-name. Here's to broken engagements. Here's to being a girl." Only we didn't do that because Edie'd made other arrangements. "You're going to have dinner with Gerald and me. The three of us will go out for dinner. My Monarose must approve of the man I'm going to marry."

Someday Edie would get married. I knew that. On a flight to Mecca she'd meet a Saudi sheik. During some turbulence, he'd pop the question, and Edie would say, "Yes, yes. I want to live out my days in a harem." From her oasis-side tent, Edie would write me long letters, smuggling them out, flipping coins as bribes to young Bedouin boys. She'd enclose snapshots of herself wearing midnight-blue chiffon pants. Then, no doubt, there'd come the day she'd have had a bellyful of fingerbells. From a lounge chair by the swimming pool, while munching figs, Edie would dispatch a cable: AM BLOWING THIS HOLE STOP WIRE CASH STOP EDIE.

Even if she had hitched up with Boris, residing in a flat off Red Square, she'd still be my Edie. And if she'd married George and lived with him at his nonexistent address, we would not have lost sight of each other.

Gerald's chair was pulled close to Edie's, joining them at the hip. Cemented together. Siamese twins of love. He had one arm around her and seemed reluctant to let go. But he stood up and extended a hand. "Geraldo," he introduced himself, like he was some smoothie from Buenos Aires. "So," Gerald sat back down, arm in place, "tell

104

me a little something about yourself." as if this were the first he'd heard of me.

"What don't you know?" I asked.

"I don't know a thing about you. What do you do for a living?"

"Hasn't Edie told you? We do this and that. Nothing serious."

He tsk-tsked at me. "Don't you think it's time you got serious?"

"When is it time to get serious? When the big hand's on the eight and the little hand hits twelve?"

"You have to get serious or you get eaten up." Gerald gave me the kind of pep talk you'd hear at a seminar for used-car salesmen. "Competition is the name of the game."

"We've been managing nicely." I looked to Edie for confirmation, but she was busy polishing off the remains of her drink.

"Someday," Gerald went on, "you're going to have to take on responsibilities. Like marriage. I've got two to care for now. Don't I, honey?" He punctuated his question by giving Edie's arm a little pinch. "Well, Mona, maybe I can help you out. Send some opportunity your way."

The only opportunity I was after was the opportunity to slip out of this dinner. The alternative was to drink myself sick, hoping to wake up the next morning remembering none of this. I flagged the waiter, and Gerald ordered another round for himself and Edie. "And give my fiancée's friend whatever she wants."

"Vodka and soda," I said.

"Fiancée," Edie mooned. "Doesn't that have a nice ring to it?"

"It sounds French."

"It is," Gerald let me know.

Our drinks arrived, and Edie and I both made a grab for them, taking big swallows. Gerald told the waiter he'd have filet mignon. "My fiancée will have the stuffed shrimp."

"I love shrimp," Edie piped up.

I asked for another drink.

Edie must've been previously privileged to hear the monologue Gerald recited at me. She blended in with the wallpaper and went mute while Gerald talked and talked with his mouth full. "Right now, I'm coordinating an exhibit for a major museum. I'm not at liberty to divulge which one. But it's major."

"I wasn't aware museum exhibits were top secret and classified," I said.

"Ah, there's nothing more gratifying than bringing together great artworks. That's what I'd do full-time except the money's not what I'm used to." Gerald toyed with Edie's person as if she were an accessory of his. A scarf whose fringes he might stroke or a lock of hair absentmindedly twirled on a forefinger. "My real income will be derived from the show I'm producing. Broadway."

I'd once read a newspaper account of a homeless woman who went to the A&P and shoved steaks down her blouse. When she was apprehended, no one bought her story about being hungry because she'd stolen quality food. The response was as if a hungry person would steal only bologna and a hunk of Velveeta. But if you have to steal food to eat, why not steal the very best food? And if you're going to tell lies, you might as well tell whoppers. "So," I asked Gerald, "what's this Broadway play of yours about?"

"It's a musical. Based on a comic strip." He named one from the Sunday funnies.

"Hasn't that been done before?"

"Isn't he a genius?" Edie popped out from her trance. "I told you he was a genius." And she went back under.

"Yep," he chuckled, "soon I'm going to be a very rich man. Edie won't have to work at all."

"Big deal." I pointed out Edie hardly works at all as it is.

"But look how she lives," the chucklehead said. "She has nothing."

"That's not so. She has plenty."

"Compared to who? The destitute? The down-and-outers? The first thing I'm going to do is get her the hell out of that neighborhood. I won't have my wife living in a slum."

"That slum is where you live, too," I reminded him.

"I had to live there. I was involved in labor organization. I needed to know the people. Win their trust. You have to do that from the inside."

"A revolutionary with bucks. Could anyone be more perfect for me, Monarose?" Edie's tongue was thick, pickled.

"As soon as my work with the union is complete, we're getting off of that block. I've got my eye on a little place on the Park. Seven rooms, doorman, Jacuzzi. My wife is going to have it all. You name it. Diamonds. Furs. I'll take her to places she never dreamed of going."

"Edie's already been everywhere worth going to. Edie," I said, "didn't you show him your map?"

Edie got the waiter's attention and motioned for a fresh drink.

"Yep," Gerald crossed his arms over his chest. "I can't wait to marry this woman. I wish we could do it tomorrow."

"Oh, Monarose. Don't you just love a boy who'll rise to an occasion?"

"Not when it's hot air propelling him up," I muttered.

Edie laughed, somewhat on the hysterical side. "Isn't she funny, Gerald?"

"Edie," I asked, "how many drinks have you had?"

"Hey, what are you? Her mother?" Gerald said Edie was fine. "Leave her alone. Let her drink what she wants."

"So fine. I couldn't be finer," Edie hiccupped.

When the check came, Gerald glanced at his watch. "Jeez, I've got to call my lawyer." He excused himself from the table and went to the men's room. We were expected to believe he was on the phone.

"His lawyer?" My eyebrows went up. "I thought you only call a lawyer at this time of night if you've been arrested."

"Oh, he's always on the phone to that lawyer of his. Wheeling and dealing." Edie teetered in her seat. "It's so darling. It's how entrepreneurs work."

"It's also how con artists operate."

"Oh, that's true, isn't it? How cute! My husband the con artist. That would be a howl, wouldn't it?"

"Not for long," I said. "And not if it's you he's conning." Not that Edie could ever be conned.

Gerald returned from the bathroom to find the check still face down on the tray. He turned it over and studied it gravely. "Let's see, Mona. Your half comes to . . ."

"My third, you mean." Quibbling over a dinner bill was not my style. I wasn't comfortable doing it, but no way was I going to let him pull a fast one on me.

"One thing you should know," he said. "In the world of high finance, a few dollars here and there is embarrassing to mention."

"I will not have my husband-to-be and my Monarose bickering over a check." Edie put her Visa card down on the tray. Gerald handed the whole package to the waiter.

I was waiting for my coffee to drip when Edie called. She wanted my opinion of Gerald.

"You must have a hangover and a half," I dodged the question.

"What did you think?" Edie asked again.

"Hard to tell," my voice squeaked. "First impressions, you know."

"Come on, Monarose. You've never been one to shy away from a snap judgment. Did you like him or not?"

If Edie were to dump Gerald on my say-so, she'd carry

around doubts like BBs, small pellets of ammunition. Not very dangerous but they could get under my skin. "He seemed okay," I lied.

"I want the truth." Edie sounded serious.

"For real. I liked him."

"Not for real, Monarose. I want the truth. I'm going to marry him, but I need to know what you think. So did you like him or not?"

"Not," I said.

"I didn't think so." After a pause, Edie asked another question. "Do you think he loves me."

I assumed Edie was looking for a loophole here, the trap door she was waiting for me to open. I aimed to help her and said, "No, he doesn't love you. He doesn't even know who you are."

"I see," she said, and she went cold. A girl ought not to ask for the truth when she doesn't really want to hear it.

"What do you see?" I asked.

"I see," she repeated, but would say no more. Nor would she hang up. She kept me on the line in limbo, a very disturbing place to be. "Let go, Edie," I said. "Whack off my hand or cut out my tongue." I opted for a swift punishment. "But let up on me. I'm sorry if that wasn't the truth you wanted, but it was the only one I knew."

When Werner called Edie and said, "I vant to zee you. I'm leaving on ze 27th," Edie said, "What a coincidence. I'm getting married on the 27th." She cut the connection.

Werner did not call back, but he sent her a box of chocolates with a note enclosed.

"What'd the note say?" I asked.

"It doesn't matter now," Edie said. "What piffle. He thinks he can win me back with a few lousy bonbons."

"But you loved the Kraut. You can't stop loving him just because you got engaged."

"Who I love is irrelevant. Who loves *me* is what counts." Edie refused to discuss this any further. All I could do was pretend Gerald, and the difficulties he was causing, didn't exist. "Finish your coffee," I said. "Let's forget about boys for the moment. Let's go out for lunch."

"I'll have to pass," Edie declined my invitation. "Gerald will be over soon. We have loads to do."

"Such as?" I asked. There was never anything Edie *had* to get done.

"I'm getting married." She indulged the urge to remind me.

"So, you're getting married. You get a license. You go to City Hall. The whole shebang doesn't take an hour."

"I'm going to have a wedding," Edie told me.

"A wedding? With a ceremony and a party and bluebells and crummy music?" I made no attempt to mask the horror.

"We decided we want one," she said.

"When?" I asked. "When did we decide that? We decided no such thing."

"Gerald and I want a wedding. Not a huge wedding. A small one. An afternoon affair. Tasteful."

Tasteful and *wedding* create an oxymoron. Even weddings which appear elegant contain at least one tacky detail. Like matchbooks with the bride and groom's name embossed, as if the happy couple were a motel or an auto school. "You never wanted a wedding," I noted. "You always said you'd elope."

"Well, I've changed my mind," Edie said. "After all, it is going to be the most memorable day of my life."

"Come off it. You've had scads of most memorable days."

"Not like this one. Not like my wedding day. Gerald wants me to have my day as a bride."

Gerald must've had visions of envelopes coming his way, envelopes containing money. "How gracious of him," I said.

"I want a wedding," she said. "To remember the day by."

"Yeah. Otherwise you might forget."

"I thought you'd understand, Monarose."

"I thought I did," I said. "I thought I understood it all. I thought I was the one who understood everything about you." I felt panicky, as if I were losing my grip on something. "But I don't understand a wedding. Weddings are dopey. You always said that. Why don't you take a trip around the world instead? I'd understand if you took a trip around the world."

"I'm going to get married. I'm going to have a wedding," Edie spoke to me in her soft and nasty voice. "Can you understand that, Monarose?"

PREPARATIONS FOR A WEDDING

7

When things go terribly wrong, some people continue about their business as usual. There are women who, each morning, set places at the table, pour coffee and corn flakes, for husbands who've long since run off with seventeen-year-old go-go dancers. Chimpanzees have been observed toting a dead baby around for weeks, fixing it at their breasts, as if it were only sleeping. And I persisted in talking to Edie as if she were still my Edie, my friend, while she deliberated between parchment and vellum for wedding invitations.

"So you see what I mean?" she said. "It's an awkward situation."

"I'm sorry. I wasn't listening," I told her. "I was think-ing about the paper dilemma."

Edie reexplained how her Aunt Jackie had sent a two-slice toaster as an engagement gift. That wouldn't do. Gerald's toast would grow cold waiting for Edie's toast to pop up. "I don't know what my aunt was thinking. Two-slice toasters are for single people. What should I do?"

I recycled this conversation because I could not accept it as it was. I answered her in my own fashion. "There can only be true love in the face of adversity. And a toaster doesn't qualify as adversity unless you stick a fork in it."

"Hmmm," Edie pondered. "I think I'm going to go with the vellum. Ecru vellum."

Edie picked up the phone and called the printer to place her order for ecru vellum invitations, and I let myself out, unsure if I could even find my way home. I was very confused.

You once knew a girl and this girl said, "*Compromise* is the only obscene word in the English language." This girl lived by the edict that the only truly wicked deed is to sell out your own soul. Yet this girl who decorated her bathroom in soap scum is suddenly covetous of mono-grammed towels. What can you do about this? You can call her up and refresh her memory. "I need to tell you something," I said.

"Make it fast." Edie had an appointment with a caterer. "I can't decide whether to have shrimp puffs or shrimp cocktail. What do you think?"

I said I thought I had the wrong number and hung up.

So you thought you knew a girl, but perhaps you were mistaken. You expected a distinct brand of style from her, but she didn't want to know about that. Some awful boy proposed they spend eternity together, and in no time flat, it grew difficult to distinguish her from a host of other girls.

I wondered just how wicked it is to sell someone else's soul down the Nile right along with your own.

"You're my best friend," Edie said. "I want you to be my attendant. But only on the condition that you're happy for me. I want you to be happy for me, Mona."

"Mona? Mona?" I'd been abridged like a *Reader's Digest* article. "Mona? Well, not that Mona isn't a nice name because it's a very nice name, but Monarose is a flower of a name."

"Don't do that," Edie said.

She was right. It was pitiful. I should've just called her Edith and been done with her. But how could I be done with her? I did not want to imagine me without Edie. I could not imagine me without Edie, and so I made a show of giving in. "Okay, okay," I said. "I'm happy for you."

The attendant's chores didn't amount to much. Edie's wedding wasn't going to be a full-blown one, thus sparing me from having to throw a crepe-paper bridal shower. I would not have to fill miniature white plastic umbrellas with jelly beans to pass out as party favors. Because she was not going to wear a gown and veil, there'd be no afternoons spent sitting on ersatz Louis XIV chairs while a buxom lady, with pins in her mouth, draped cloth around Edie, as if wrapping her for the sarcophagus. Really, all that was being asked of me was that I give Edie away. And, oh yes, be happy about it.

In Saks, we got on the escalator going up. Edie told me to keep my eyes peeled for anything in white silk.

"White?" I smirked.

"Yes. Isn't that what brides traditionally wear?"

"So I've heard," I said.

"I want to be married in a white silk dress."

"Why not get married in something wash 'n' wear?" I suggested. "That way you can use it over and over again."

We stepped off the escalator and over to the racks of silk dresses, those zero sorts of dresses sold by the yard, worn with a single strand of pearls.

Edie was a lot more choosy when it came to picking a dress than she was about picking a husband. Two, three times she tried on every white, off-white, ivory, and egg-shell dress in the store. Finally she settled on the ivory scoop-necked one. We got on line to pay for it, and she asked again, "You're sure it's not too daring?"

"I'm positive." Boring, maybe. But daring that dress was not. I flipped up the price tag and gasped. "Edie, this dress costs as much as a plane ticket to Moscow."

"So what?" she said. "A girl only gets married once in her life."

And I wanted to know since when.

The saleswoman wrapped Edie's dress in tissue. Edie wrote out a check. I stared at the floor. A snippet of green maribou feather drifted along the carpet. This made me think, what if Edie had indeed succeeded in astrally projecting herself to the Kremlin as she once planned? What if the night before meeting Gerald, she made the trip over but couldn't find her way back? Taking advantage of Edie's absence, some lost bit of fluff inhabited her body the way a hermit crab will move into an empty snail's shell. Poor Edie, destined to drift while the bit of fluff paraded around in her body, making a muck of her life.

"A stunning dress." The saleswoman handed Edie the shopping bag.

"Thank you," Edie said. "It's going to be my wedding dress. I'm getting married."

Edie wanted shoes to match the dress. Shoes were on the same floor as lingerie. We had a serious affection for lingerie. Once, after spending two weeks' worth of food money on a wisp of lace, I'd lamented, "Oh, Edie, what have I done? Pretty as this is, I can't live on it." And Edie said, "Don't be silly. Of course you can live on it. Food can always be had. Nourishment for the spirit is hardest to come by."

Leaving Edie to try on satin pumps, I scooted over to the stocking display. There I fingered the samples in silk. Silk stockings are luscious, a whisper of a cool breeze rolling across the skin. So expensive, and rarely do they last through the event they were intended for. Silk stockings struck me as the perfect wedding gift for Edie. She'd have no use for a Waterford candy dish. And what would she do with a vacuum other than, perhaps, to live in one? She'd like silk stockings best. I had the saleswoman wrap up a half-dozen pairs.

I found Edie amid a sea of shoeboxes. "For you," I gave her the package. "Your wedding present."

Edie opened my gift. "Stockings?" she said.

"Silk stockings," I told her.

"What kind of wedding gift is that?" she asked. "You're supposed to give china and crystal and appliances. You know that."

"No," I said. "I don't know anything of the kind."

After shopping, I went back to Edie's apartment for a cup of coffee. On the table was a stack of travel brochures. I picked one up and asked, "Planning a trip?"

"Yes," she said. "A honeymoon."

"How quaint. Where to?" A reflex action, I looked over to her map, the one with the red circles on it. It was gone. In place were the thumbtacks pinning torn scraps of blue paper, corners of oceans, to the wall. The patch where Edie's world had once been was whiter than the space around it, as if that spot had been sun-bleached by a beam of light.

Edie and Gerald were going to honeymoon in the Pocono Mountains. That sounded a bit more like my Edie, choosing to honeymoon in a tacky stucco motel with vibrating beds, pink heart-shaped bathtubs, and porn flicks on the television.

"Not that sort of place." Edie said I had it all wrong. "We'll be staying at a country inn."

"Oh, Edie," I pleaded, "go for the mirrors on the ceiling and Cold Duck in the fridge." I wanted, needed, her to make a mockery of this. "That's what I'd do," I challenged.

"But I'm not you," Edie said. "And you're not me."

That wasn't quite accurate. She forgot that when she met me I was a blank slate, an empty canvas she painted with many colors. In a way, I was her creation. We were as much one as an artist and her art.

If Edie were so bent on having a wedding, she might've gone whole hog with horse-drawn carriages, coronets, dozens of handmaidens. She could've donned one of those cone hats with a trailing chiffon scarf. Or she might've been married in a pigpen by a justice of the peace who doubled as the town drunk. Had she done that, I could've said, "Well, you know Edie." Instead, she picked to be married in the United Nations chapel. Nearly everyone has a cousin who got married there. It's where you have your wedding if the Botanical Gardens is booked. Our past infatuation with the United Nations had to do with espionage, intrigue, foreign affairs—not the namby-pamby goodwill the chapel represented.

"It's a nice chapel," Edie said. "Unitarian."

"Unitarian?" Edie wasn't Unitarian.

"We're going with Ceremony Number Four," she told me. They'd been offered six ceremonies to choose from, variations of poems and slogans, like a combination plate, one from Column A and two from Column B.

"It sounds like a game show," I remarked. "What's behind Ceremony Number Two? If you get your lines wrong, does the minister squirt seltzer in your face? Can you win big cash prizes and Samsonite luggage?"

"Cut it out." Edie bit off the tail end of a smile. "It's not a dreadful ceremony. Some of them," she confided, "were ridiculous."

The waitress set down our coffee, and when she went off, I asked Edie, "You're not really going through with this, are you? It's a hoax, isn't it?"

"Someone loves me enough to marry me. And so I'm going to marry him. It's no hoax, Mona."

I let Edie know who it was she was trying to fool. "You're up to something. I can sense it." More likely, it was hope I was experiencing, not intuition.

Edie shrugged. "Maybe I am up to something. Then again, maybe I'm not. No one really knows the future, do they?"

I let Edie's dig pass. "Come on, what's the scheme?" I asked. "Maybe I can help."

"You can't help because there is no scheme. I might not know what the future holds exactly, but I am going to go through with this wedding. I'm going to marry Gerald. I'm going to start fitting in," she said.

"Like the square peg in the round hole," I laughed.

120

Edie did not laugh. "I'm tired," she said. "I want what other girls have. I've always wanted what other girls had, only I didn't know how to get it. When we first met," she said, "I wanted to be just like you were. Very normal. I was hoping you'd teach me. But you didn't."

"You didn't want that, Edie. You scorned it. All the way, you scorned it."

"I'm going to marry Gerald," she repeated.

"Why? Tell me why, Edie?" I might've been begging, but I couldn't help myself. This was like watching her surrender. No, worse. It was watching her fall out of love.

"I want a husband," she said. "I want to be safe and happy. I want to be just like everyone else."

"You'll never be like everyone else. You're much better than that."

"I don't want to be better," Edie said. "I want to be the same."

"You can't be the same. You're different," I insisted.

"I can be however I want, Mona. And what I want is to no longer be your entertainment. I am sick of being the source of amusement."

"Oh?" I got indignant. "The source of amusement, huh? Let me tell you something, Edie. You're not always so amusing. Or entertaining. Sometimes you were a pain. Demanding. Difficult. Sometimes I wanted to shake you because . . ." I didn't get to tell her that it was, on occasion, draining to go along as if on stage, a key player in a full-blown theatrical production with fan dancers, jugglers, and no intermission. That now and then, I got dirty cleaning up after her. That there were times when I wanted to sit down on solid ground and scream, Stop! But all those times put together amounted to a wisp of nothing when stacked up against how happy I was, how lovely it was.

But Edie didn't let me get to that part. "Good," she said. "Then you're as relieved as I am that it's over."

"I went along with you. On all of it. I bought into your whole story."

"You didn't do a damn thing you didn't want to do. Face it, Mona. As much as I wanted to be you, you wanted to be me. And you got what you were after, but I didn't."

"You're making a big mistake." My hand shot out to hold her back.

"Quit trying to wreck my life." Edie threw some money down, and she was gone.

Going home held no appeal. So I walked over to 23rd Street to visit Fawn. I first met Fawn when I worked as a photographer's assistant. That job lasted seven weeks. Powdering teenage noses for high school yearbook shots was not as glamorous as I'd imagined it'd be. Fawn was in charge of lighting.

So very pleased that I stopped by, Fawn swept me inside. She flitted about making me comfortable. While she whipped up refreshments, I leafed through a magazine and mentioned I was a bit out of sorts. "Edie's been treating me pretty shabbily."

Fawn poured tea without caffeine into mugs without handles. "Hmph, Edie. Really, Mona, this is the best thing that could happen for you. I don't know if you realize this, but Edie is not a very nice person."

122

I shook my head. "You don't really know her, Fawn."

"Frankly," Fawn took a sip of tea, "from the first time I met her, I could see right through her."

Frankly, Fawn couldn't see right through air.

She passed me a plate of kelp or sawdust and told me my friendship with Edie was based on blind loyalty. "Now, loyalty is very admirable, but there can be too much of a good thing."

"No, there can't be," I disagreed. "There's never too much when it's good." More lame than Fawn's inability to get my drift was my attempting to explain it to her. "See, when I'm with Edie, humdrum is just a ringing in the ears. What was otherwise plain became exalted because she said it was exalted."

Fawn was scandalized. "You believe everything she says? Come on, Mona. You're too smart for that."

"I believe everything Edie says because she makes it true even when it's not." Like she made me believe I was enigmatic and enchanting when I wasn't anyone special.

"You mean to tell me if Edie said it were safe to jump off the Empire State Building, you'd believe that?"

"Yes," I said, "because if Edie and I jumped from the Empire State Building, our parachutes would open, and we'd drift lazily to the ground."

"I'm not following you." Fawn wore the same expression on her face as a sparrow who has flown down the chimney and discovered itself in a living room.

"Look, Fawn, before I knew Edie I was afraid of life. I was a shy, timid, nice girl."

123

"Yes," Fawn said heartily. "And you could be again. Without her, you're perfectly nice."

"I don't want to be perfectly nice. I never wanted to be perfectly nice. Only I lacked the nerve, the guts, the daring to be anything but a nice girl whose life was pretty well mapped out for her. Edie gave me the courage to step off the path, to stray wherever I desired, to be a noteworthy girl living an uncommon life."

Fawn cringed at the word *girl*. "Woman," she said. "We're women. Not girls."

"Oh, Fawn. Please try to understand what it means to have every inconsequential act be wondrous simply because you want it to be."

"But that's distorted. That's not how life is," Fawn said, cluing me in on one of her empirical truths.

"I know it's distorted," I said. "That's the beauty of it."

All sad stories are about lost illusions. Lost illusions are not the same thing as getting hurt. When you get hurt, you recover. Especially if you're young. Youth is resilient. But once an illusion is gone, it's gone for good. Youth is not a consideration because it goes the instant the illusion is lost.

"Don't cry," Fawn said gently to me.

"I'm not crying."

"Mona, you're not being realistic."

"I know that. It was a choice. I had a choice. I didn't want to be realistic when I had the other."

Taking my hand, Fawn meant to be kind. "I'll try, if

you want. If you tell me what to do and say, I'll try being unrealistic with you."

Fawn waited for me to explain, step by step, how to make fancy from nothingness, while I learned exactly how irreplaceable Edie was.

A box of bonbons might've been a paltry offering, but the final-hour act of a desperate man is always dashing. With Werner's aid, this wedding could be stopped. He'd do whatever it took because I'd order him to. If Germans are famous for one thing, it's doing as they're told. Besides, he loved her.

Pressing a five-spot on the doorman, I asked him if he'd be so kind as to get me a cab. So near to rush hour, I'd have a good ten minutes to find Werner.

As "my Kraut" had suited Edie's purposes of identification, I didn't know Werner's full name, so I scouted the mailboxes for names that were German. There was a Schmitt in 2B and a Kreuzner in 7E. I got in the elevator and pressed 7. I knew some Schmitts. They were from Cleveland.

Apartment E was at the end of the hall. The doorbell chimed. I didn't have a speech prepared. I figured the Kraut and I would take one look at each other and speak a universal language. He might cry. I'd tell him to pull himself together and polish his boots. We have things to do.

Ingrid opened the door. She was wearing tight jeans

and a *New York New York* sweatshirt. I looked past her and saw row upon row of packing crates lined up in size order.

My nerve was draining fast. I was about to say I had the wrong apartment when Werner called out, "Who is zere, Ingrid?"

"Immigration," I snapped. "I must see Mr. Kreuzner. Mr. Werner Kreuzner."

Ingrid eyed me with suspicion. Werner stepped into the threshold and paled. "Mr. Kreuzner," I tried to sound official. "I'm from Immigration. I need to have a word with you. Privately."

Reluctantly, Ingrid allowed Werner to step past her into the hallway. He pulled the door closed behind him. "Vhy are you here? Zis is no goot."

"You're damn right this is no good. Yes or no, Werner, do you love Edie or not?"

"Yes, but . . ."

"No buts. If you love her, you've got to act. Do something big. Cancel your plans. Quit your job. Stay here. We can't let her go through with this wedding."

"Edie is a grown voman."

"No, she's not. She's marrying out of spite. She loves you. And you love her. Come with me. Declare yourself and your intentions."

Werner was shaking his head. "Mona, my intentions are to go back inside and finish ze packing."

"But you love her."

"I have things I must do."

126

I hung around long enough to hear him tell Ingrid, "Nothing. It vas nothing."

The doorman was still at the corner trying to flag me a cab. "Forget it," I said to him. "There's no point to it anymore."

After six hours of staring at my ceiling, I went out for a pack of cigarettes. When I got back, the phone was ringing. As if I'd summoned him via the cosmic airwaves, it was George. "You heard me calling you," I said because I wanted him to be a bonafide miracle.

George played dumb, claiming he'd only called to say hello. "I'm in town for a few weeks. I wanted to get together."

"Oh, sure. This week of all weeks you happen to breeze by. Years pass and not even a postcard from you, but now you happen to be in town."

"Is there something I should know about?" George continued to feign ignorance. I played along. Still, I kept the explanation brief, believing it redundant; he'd already heard it all through the celestial grapevine. "You will stop her, won't you? That is why you're here?"

George asked if I ever tried to stop a freight train with my foot.

"She loved you, George. She loved you very much. She'd love you again. Marry her, George. Please marry her."

"I'd sooner marry a tarantula," George said.

127

"Help me stop her," I pleaded. "Please. Come up with a plan. I don't want to lose Edie."

"I don't know why not." But George did agree to think of something. "Arrange to have dinner with her tomorrow night. Do not, I repeat, *do not* mention me. You and I will arrive early. She'll come to meet you, and I'll be there to surprise her."

"And then what?"

"I don't know yet," he said. "But something will happen."

Edie wasn't keen on having dinner with me until I said, "It's your bachelorette party. You have to have one. It's tradition. After dinner, we'll go to a male strip joint." I also implied there'd be gifts for her. "The Blue Mill at eight," I said.

"The Blue Mill? We haven't been there since . . ."

I put a stop to speculation. "I'm in the mood for their onion soup."

Edie spotted George and faltered, as if considering not coming to the table. When she did, in lieu of "Hello," or "Where the hell have you been for the last thousand years?" Edie said, "I'm getting married."

"So I've heard." George's voice was honey-laced. "And when is the big day?"

Reaching into her purse, Edie took out an invitation. She carried a stack of invitations around with her and passed them out like business cards. "Day after tomorrow," she said. "You're invited."

128

George raised his glass. "To your happiness." Then, rapid-fire, George aimed questions at her. He asked where they'd be honeymooning? And living? And working? And how soon before she started breeding? And would they spend holidays with his family or hers?

This was clever, forcing her to look at the whole ugly picture in one sitting, like reality immersion.

"As long as you're happy," George said.

Edie shot him a look and said, "At least I know where this boy lives."

George gave me a thumbs-up. If she were really happy, she wouldn't be holding a grudge against George merely because years ago he gave her the suicide hotline as his phone number.

Timing is essential in the execution of a good scheme. George knew precisely when to switch gears. "I have some lovely gossip if you'd care for some," he said, knowing fully well Edie could've eaten gossip every day for lunch and grown plump on the juice. "That girl we knew in school, the one who ate Valium like they were salted peanuts."

"Elise Fromberg," Edie volunteered the name.

"Yes," said George. "Somehow she landed a job with one of the networks. Assistant director of game show programming."

"That's the gossip?" Edie was disappointed.

"No. That's the prelude to the gossip. Anyway, television programming is a stressful occupation. She was under a lot of pressure. One day, to relax, she gobbled a few too many pills and insisted on being the 5000-dollar bonus question. She burst onto the set and demanded, 'Who am I?' And one of the contestants guessed Anastasia Romanov."

"We have some gossip, too, George," Edie said. "We heard you were in Liechtenstein. Mona ran into that goofy boy who saw you there."

"He was mistaken. I've never been to Liechtenstein."

"Then where have you been? And how is it you happen to show up now?" Edie looked at me as if I had a hand in this.

"I missed you," George grinned.

"That's a lie," Edie said. "You never missed me. Everything you say is a lie." She stood up, fresh drink in hand, and emptied the glass over George's head.

For one bright twinkle, I thought we had our Edie back.

"You're uninvited to my wedding." She snatched her invitation away. "I won't let you ruin my chance at a nice life. Either of you." Edie brushed past the waiter carrying our dinners.

With vodka and soda dripping from his hair, George told me a story. "This was when I knew Edie less than a week. I was coming from my Milton seminar. I was walking up the same corridor Edie happened to be walking down. She was smiling at me, so full of fun and laughter. It appeared she was delighted to see me, so I stopped, arms outstretched to hug her. As she came in close, she reached into her jacket and pulled out a gun. A water gun. And she shot me in the eye. And sometimes I can still feel it," George flicked away some of Edie's drink, "right where she shot me with that water gun."

George paid the bill and asked me what was the appropriate tip in America.

"Why did you lie about Liechtenstein, George?"

"I didn't lie. I wasn't in Liechtenstein. I was in another small and rich banking country. The boy you met was confused. He'd been traveling a lot. You know how people get confused on a whirlwind tour."

George walked with me to Ross's apartment. Sirens wailed in the night. Police. Ambulances. Burglar alarms. Fire trucks. Catastrophes galore. "You're better than she is," George said. "She knew that. She fed off you."

"Why, then, are we so grim?" I asked.

"We're not grim." George did a two-step, a skip that was meant to be joyous. It flopped.

"I feel like somebody died," I told him.

"Somebody did."

"Yeah, and I think it's me. Do I look dead, George?"

"No. You look beautiful."

"So suffering is good for the complexion after all, eh?"

At Ross's doorway, I said good-night to George. "Thanks for trying."

Ross let me in and asked, "How'd it go?"

"Not well," I said. "I'm not up to the task. Edie is the only person I know who is capable of stopping a wedding. How's that for irony?"

Ross poured me a brandy. "Drink this. You'll feel better."

131

"No, I won't feel better," I took a swallow. "I feel lost. I can't accept this, Ross."

"You're making too much of it. Friends come. Friends go."

"Edie isn't just a friend."

"Oh, then what is she?" Ross was considering, and warming to, the possibility that Edie might've been my lover.

"Forget that, Ross. It's not that way. It's that she's my other half. More than my other half. My three quarters. My seven eighths. Without her, I'm only a shadow."

Ross put his arm around me and pulled me close. "You feel like plenty more than a shadow to me," he said.

I didn't want anyone touching me. I broke away and said, "I know what's happening. Now all I have to do is face it. Face my destiny."

"And what is that?" Ross made light.

"That these last years have been an attempt to evade fate. But you can't evade fate. And my fate is to be a pleasant enough woman who marries a dentist, drops a couple of kids, lives in a colonial-style house like the one I grew up in. That is my destiny, Ross. There is no place in my stars for this catch-as-catch-can life. Nor," I added, "for any romance with a fifty-year-old musician."

"What dentist? Who are you talking about?"

"I don't know," I said. "I haven't met him yet. But I will. He might not be a dentist. He could be a CPA. Or a tax man. Maybe I'll meet him at Edie's wedding."

"Finish your brandy." Ross picked up the glass and held it out to me.

132

"I don't want any brandy." I headed for the door.

"Where are you going?" Ross asked. "What's happening here?"

"It's over, Ross. All of it, everything, is over."

"Over with us? Is that what you mean?"

I said yes, that too. I suppose I should've felt sad about Ross. I was kind of wild about him. But I was too miserable to feel sad.

"Listen," Ross tried to keep me back, "why don't you sleep on it, okay? Things will look different in the morning."

"No, Ross. In the morning," I said, "there will only be more light on the same subject."

ACCOMMODATE THE DAY

8

The only effective recourse for insomnia is surrender. So I get up from my bed, make coffee, and drag my armchair to the window. I look out facing east.

I'll sit here awhile contemplating choices.

Once I loved a boy whose goal was to visit every sea. Whenever a city was mentioned, he'd ask, "What sea is that on?" and he'd write it down. Given the time zones, right about now he's probably taking tea and scones on a balcony overlooking the Caspian. I could join him there.

Or I could rubber-raft down rivers. Float from the Danube to the Rhine, cut into a tributary to the Seine, eventually wind up bobbing down the Hudson, and home.

Or I could fly to Athens. See if the gods have returned. Have lunch with them and send Edie a telegram hand-delivered by Achilles: SO SORRY STOP COULDN'T MAKE IT STOP BEST WISHES STOP. Then I'd wile away the remainder of the afternoon with Hera and the girls. In a café on the plakka, we'd sip lemonade from golden straws and snicker over my silly friend and her foolish mortal ways.

Or I could go to Edie's wedding and catch the bouquet.

I light a cigarette. A band of pink cuts across the horizon. Dawn is reputed to be a romantic event, but it's too predictable. Real romance is never an everyday occurrence. Yet pairs of people are spooning over this slop as if the sun rose for them alone.

Pink makes way for yellow. The sky looks like a Lilly Pulitzer dress.

The night we graduated from college, Edie and I went to the Plaza Hotel and got tanked on drinks decorated with paper parasols. Weaving our way to the fountain, we pitched coins into the pool and vowed we'd be friends forever. After tossing in our last nickels and dimes, we walked to the Village. Edie bitched because her shoes pinched, but we walked the whole way regardless. We wanted that night to last forever, too. Also, we walked because we hadn't any money left. We'd spent it all on mai tais and promises.

135

Forever. So just how long is forever in America? Three minutes, enough time to boil an egg? A couple of weeks? Nine years? Are you supposed to stick around to watch it end?

Rice. Of course, rice. Tossing rice at Edie will speak volumes, all the words I'd never say. And Edie will know exactly what it means. Surely I'll be the only one to remember to toss rice at the bride. Everyone else will have forgotten that.

I know I have some Uncle Ben's around here someplace. But where? It's not in the kitchen cabinets. They're as bare as Old Mother Hubbard's. Nor do I find rice in the freezer or my desk drawer. The box turns up on a bookshelf wedged behind Bartlett's *Quotations*. I blow the dust from it.

Smoothing an old silk handkerchief out flat, I pour a handful of rice into the center. The way I've witnessed baby diaperings, I bring up the corners. The ends get knotted together to make a pouch. Through the cloth, I finger the grains of rice. No two are bound together.

My bathroom walls are flamingo pink. The pale pink I'd picked out went on like hot neon. It never did fade with time like most things do. Edie'd been after me to plant a palm tree in here, and scatter around empty oyster shells. "Make it look like a little piece of Miami," she said.

I turn on the taps and run a bath.

136

My red toenails peek out above the white bubbles. There's not another friend in the world for me. I know this. As if expecting to hit a hard surface, I bring my fist down. It splashes the water, and soap stings my eyes.

No one can see me. No one will ever find out. And so what if they did? A girl ought to be able to have a small cry in the privacy of her bath.

It's in poor taste to wear black to weddings. It's reputed to bring bad tidings or the seven-year itch or some such thing. What would be appropriate is some swishy dress the same color as a fruit, but I don't have any dresses like that. I'll have to chipper up a black dress with pearls or a scarf in lemon or apricot.

Slipping on a black sheath, I go to the mirror. The effect is somber, like I'm about to throw myself on top of a fresh grave. This is definitely the thing to wear should I plan on being dragged, wailing, from a cemetery. I take it off and go back to my closet.

A suit might do. A suit with this azure-blue blouse, ruffles at the neck and cuffs. Someone must've given me this blouse. I never would've bought something with ruffles.

I hook my stockings to my garters and step into my shoes.

Without makeup, I might as well be naked. I powder my face, rim my eyes with kohl. My lips get outlined in burgundy and filled in with scarlet. A coat of gloss, and my mouth looks kissable. I sweep up my hair, pinning it

137

in a knot. Not a dour knot, but fixed just enough to imply it'll tumble.

I turn this way and that, and I catch, in the mirror, what my admirers will not. Something's missing. A quality. A spark. No longer flushed with anticipation, I resemble a Christmas tree on the 26th of December.

The telephone rings and, with a glimmer of hope, I answer it. It's Henry Cosgrove after a hot tip. Our crowd, he tells me, is gaming on the outcome of the wedding.

Henry says it's like a football pool. "Ten dollars to pick the date you think Edie will fly the coop. Whoever comes closest wins the pot. Minus the house cut, of course." Henry mentions the pot is amounting to a substantial sum.

The odds-on favorite is two days. Come first thing Monday morning, they're wagering, Edie will be on line at divorce court. While at one time I, too, would've plunked my ten-spot on the favorite, I now tell Henry, "I wouldn't bet on anything."

"Ah, Mona, don't hold out on me." Henry believes I've got the inside scoop. "I want to finance a car with this."

"Honest, Henry. I don't know."

As if I were stringing him along, Henry says, "All right. We'll play it your way. I'll put up the front money. You give me the straight dope, and we'll split the winnings. What do you say?"

"There's no way of knowing."

"Then guess," Henry directs.

"My guess is she'll stay married forever."

"Mona, please. Get real. No one stays married forever anymore."

"You know how stubborn Edie is," I remind him. "There's no telling what she'll do."

"Good-bye car," Henry says.

"Don't feel bad," I tell him. "You don't want a car. You drink too much to have a car."

"Yeah, I suppose you're right," Henry consoles himself. "Still, we should get something out of this. Let's go for the even money. An outright bet. If we agree Edie's going to remain married for an indeterminate period, then we have to assume she is, indeed, going to get married today. There's some talk around that this wedding is a prank. So we wager on her being there with someone who thinks she won't."

This kind of talk brings a picture to mind: the organist pumping out "Here Comes the Bride" while Edie is surveying the departure schedule at Kennedy's International terminal. That Fluffy thing draped around her neck, her cream-colored suitcase strapped to a cart, she deliberates whether to go to Bali or Gdansk.

"So you're positive she's going to get married today?" Henry repeats.

The sky is clear blue, cloudless. The temperature is balmy. As Edie won't accommodate the day, the day could at least accommodate us. The day ought to bring a storm with black clouds, ominous clouds outlined in eerie yellow. It is hurricane season in many parts of the world. Some people are getting monsoons while I'm stuck in a gentle cross-breeze. If I were in control of such matters, I'd conjure up an earthquake, a volcano, a tornado. A great twister lifting us up and carting us off to Kansas, where Edie could find romance in the flatness of the terrain and passion in the cornfields. Instead, we've got this perfect spring day. The whole damn city will be lightheaded with joy.

I turn into the candy store. Behind the counter, Frank puts down the racing form.

"Dunhills," I tell him. "Three packs of Dunhills."

"What? No Camel Lights? For the last two years it's been Camel Lights. Now you're gonna switch brands on me?"

"Three packs of Dunhills, Frank."

"Okay, okay." He slides me the cigarettes and takes my money. "So," he asks, "when's the big day?"

"We don't know, Frank. It's best to repent now." I pocket my change and put the cigarettes in my purse. Dunhills don't taste any different from other brands, but they're packaged in a jazzy red and gold box. Sometimes appearances are everything.

I drop my token in the turnstile. This is not the subway whose flashing lights will announce my arrival. Nor is it the subway of the proletariat about to rise up against oppression. It's not even the subway where the Flatbush stop looks exactly like the Austrian-Hungarian border check. It's the subway for people who haven't the imag-

ination to make it something other than what it is. It's
the subway I ride alone, on my own, and it deposits me
onto Lexington Avenue.

Although I happen to know this neck of Manhattan as
well as any, I am unaccountably lost. My bearings have
left me. I don't know which way to turn. I approach a
woman in a red jacket for directions. She is walking a
black schnauzer on a red leather leash. She knows the
value of a detail. Her directions are explicit. I thank her,
but I do not move. The woman and her dog watch me
curiously as I weigh my decision—to attend Edie's wedding or not—one last time.

AN EVENT

9

If a church isn't white clapboard modest, it ought to be monstrous with spirals, towers, gables, and ogres. A scandal or two should be buried behind clammy mortar. The United Nations chapel is neither. It takes no stand, invites no God, fierce or benevolent. I do, however, admire the revolving door offering the option of coming and going all in one roll.

The lobby walls are freshly painted white. Inoffensive pen-and-ink drawings matted in wheat hang with Holiday Inn precision. I walk from one to the next, the clickety-click of my heels is muffled. A minimum of echo, the place has good acoustics.

"Monarose, there you are."

I turn to Edie's mother. She is relieved to find me. She's nervous as a fidget and thinks I'm a cool cookie. She also thinks I'm a stablilizing influence on her daughter. Everyone has their delusions.

Edie's father, I gather, isn't going to show up, but he sent regrets by way of a big check. This will be square with Edie. She'd much rather have the money.

Mrs. Hawkes puts an arm around my waist and reminds me to call her Julia. Together we go to the attendants' chamber, a room not much bigger than a closet sandwiched between the lobby and the chapel. I sit on a metal folding chair at a cafeteria-style table, the Formica sort that doesn't stain. You can't carve your initials in it, either.

Julia fiddles with a stack of white boxes from the florist. "Your corsage." She picks at a knot in the ribbon. "But I can't get it open. My hands are shaking too much. Look." She holds them out for me to see.

The corsage is of lilacs, as is, I learn from Julia, the bridal bouquet. "I told her lilacs are for funerals, not weddings," Julia says. "But she insisted on lilacs. You know how she is once she makes up her mind."

I nod empathetically, thinking how Julia doesn't know the half of it.

"Then, try finding lilacs in March. They don't bloom until April, you know."

While putting on my corsage, I jab my finger on the pearl-studded pin. I bleed but not enough to make anything of it. Lilacs make for a dopey-looking corsage, a bunch of pale grapes hanging from my lapel.

143

"I must've called every florist in the city before finding one who could get lilacs," Julia goes on. "But Edie wouldn't hear of anything else. If she couldn't have lilacs, she would've canceled the wedding."

"Edie's fond of lilacs," I say.

"But it's too early for lilacs. Most of these buds are closed up tight." Julia sets two vases on the table and arranges the flowers expertly. This calms her. I offer to help, but she says, "No, thank you, Monarose. I need to keep busy." Edie's mother is now the only person who still calls me Monarose. I wonder if she knows it's not really my name.

After adding a few flourishes with ferns, Julia is satisfied with her floral arrangement. She carries one vase, and then the other, into the chapel. When she doesn't return promptly, I open the door and spy on Julia as she places a vase on the window sill. But she doesn't leave it there. She moves it by the front left pew before moving it again. Each time she sets the vase down, she takes three steps away and cocks her head. The other vase is smack in the middle of the aisle where the bride and groom could trip over it.

I light up a cigarette just as the minister comes in from the lobby. Edie never mentioned the minister was so handsome. I take the Dunhill from my lips and cup it in my palm in a vain attempt to hide it. The minister lights up a Marlboro.

Cigarette in one hand, he proffers the other. I put my Dunhill back between my lips. His handshake is not the limp, three-fingered clasp of a clergyman but the firm, hearty grip of a tennis partner. "Hi," he says. "I'm Steve."

I can tell this minister works hard at being hot-looking. That washboard tummy of his, rippling under his garb, didn't get that way through prayer. His well-trimmed salt-and-pepper beard bears no resemblance to any beard in the Bible.

"And you are . . . ?" Steve asks me.

"Huh?" I'm busy looking at his fingernails. They're manicured. "Oh, me. I'm Jewish," I say. I assume he was after my name or my role in this event, but because he rubs me the wrong way, I get contrary. "I'm a Jewess," I emphasize with a superior edge, like I've got a serious religion, albeit one I've neglected, and not some feather-weight trendy one.

"This is a nondenominational chapel," he tells me.

I'll bet Steve hasn't chatted with God in ages, and except for maybe once, in an impassioned teenage experience, he's never been down on his knees in his life. He is not a minister I could turn to in this hour of need.

"So you're the maid of honor?" Steve makes small talk.

"The attendant," I say.

"A lovely couple, don't you agree?"

"Who?"

"The bride and groom," he tells me.

"Oh, you mean Edie and . . ." I flip my hand around in the air like it's a fish on a boat deck.

Steve checks his expensive watch. "Yes. They ought to be here soon." With no respect for my private thoughts, Steve yaps about all the hotshot couples he's married

145

over the years. "And she made such a beautiful bride," Steve prattles on. "You've seen pictures of her, no doubt."

"No."

"Well, all brides are beautiful."

"You really think that?" I ask.

"Why yes, of course. Brides glow with happiness."

"Didn't you ever consider how the universe is so well ordered that there's a flip side to everything? Like for every joining together, there's a breaking apart? It's elementary physics," I tell him, "having to do with magnets and atoms splitting."

"To everything there is a season," Steve quotes Peter, Paul and Mary.

"Let me ask you this," I say. "Haven't you ever run into a marriage which was a mistake from the beginning? Didn't you ever want to tell some couple to forget it?"

"What kind of talk is that?" Steve chides. "Weddings are blessed events."

I blow my cigarette smoke downward, aiming for the corsage.

Steve checks his watch again. "I hope they get here shortly." Then he excuses himself. He doesn't say where he's going, so I assume it's to the bathroom.

As he exits from one door, Edie's mother flutters in through the other. Guests have begun to arrive. "Four of them are here already," Julia says. "Where's Edie?"

"She should be along any minute."

"I ought to stay in the chapel," Julia thinks aloud, "to greet the guests as they get here."

Because I can only keep a facade going at intervals, I

146

tell Julia that's a good plan. I promise to let her know the instant Edie shows up.

Well, raise high the roofbeam—it's the groom, except this groom is none too tall. Also, I can't help but notice, he shows hints of growing fat. His jacket pulls across his bottom. He kisses me on the cheek. I recognize that kiss. It's the one before the knife in the back.

"So where's my bride-to-be?" Gerald scans the chamber.

"She's not with you?" I say.

Looking over his shoulder—a regular funny guy—he says, "Nope. I don't see her. Just Jimmy here." Jimmy, I gather, is his attendant. Tall, scrawny, and freshly shaven with an old blade, Jimmy's face is raw and red from razor burn. He reminds me of a basketball player I knew in college who, when I declined to let him knead and paw at me, said, "Why not? You do it for everyone else."

Jimmy grunts some sort of greeting. I do not return the social amenities.

Stabbing my cigarette out in the tin ashtray, I grind it to bits. Gerald and I lock eyes, square off. I wouldn't be a bit surprised if he spit in his hands and ran them through his hair. He gives a cocky little laugh and goes to the mirror. His henchman follows. They preen until Steve comes in. "There's a separate chamber for you two. This one's for the ladies." Steve ushers the two goons out.

At the door, the groom turns back to me and says, "See you soon, Mona. And Mona, try smiling. You're so pretty when you smile."

Taking my compact from my purse, I check my face

for signs of aging. I feel as if I've lost resiliency. I sag in my chair, not enough bounce in me to sit up straight.

I slip the compact away because Steve comes back again. One peacock per room is plenty. "She's not here yet?" he asks. "She was supposed to be here an hour before the ceremony. Now it's almost time."

"So she'll be late. What's the rush?" I want to know.

The rush is some minor celebrities have the chapel lined up next. Steve does not want to keep them waiting. He wants to keep his celebrities happy. The rest of us can suck eggs for all he cares.

"Well," I say, "if she misses her turn, then she'll have to forfeit."

Steve looks at me as if reminding himself he is supposed to love all God's creatures. "I'm sure she'll be along any minute now," he says.

I open the door to the chapel for a quick peek. Not much of a crowd, really. From our group, I see only those with money riding on the outcome of this wedding. Plus, I spot Marissa and Fred, a duo renowned for going to any function where they can eat and drink for free.

Julia flits over and squeezes through the crack in the door. "She's here?"

"No," I shake my head.

As if they've gone to sleep on her, and she's shaking out the pins and needles, Julia wrings her hands. Through the lobby door, Steve barges in making sounds like a record skipping. "Two minutes. Two minutes. We're supposed to begin in two minutes." Doors open. Heads pop in and out. Doors close. Steve paces and repeats, "Two minutes. Two minutes." Edie's mother sails through the chamber the way a sunfish tacks. She goes to the pay phone and returns more frantic than ever. "She's not answering the phone."

"Did you call the morgue, Julia?" Edie's Aunt Jackie asks.

Gerald is not quite as smug as he was an hour ago. His upper lip holds six beads of sweat. A dark, round wet spot spreads across the back of his jacket. He won't look my way. In almost a whisper, he whines at Steve, "Where is she?"

In a stew of his own, Steve says, "Damned if I know."

I take another look into the chapel. The guests twist and turn in their seats. Hushed speculations make a roar. Money changes hands. A small charge ripples through the pews. I feel it lapping at my feet like a happy puppy. I let the door close and take my seat, the metal folding chair that's front-row center to the excitement.

Steve is patting the groom. He'll need a towel to dry his hands when he's done. Julia looks to me for an explanation. The best man is digging his pinky around in his ear. As for me, I beam. I gloat. I shine. No longer a mere bridal attendant at a sorry wedding, I'm a B-girl replete with flash cards and net stockings.

Attempting to bring calm, Steve tells us, as if he got the word from above, that Edie will be along shortly. "She's probably stuck in traffic. Let's get ourselves ready so we can start as soon as she gets here."

149

In the quiet of the postspectacle aftermath, I picture Edie foxtrotting this story, dancing it around, twirling, dipping it. She'll spin the tale of how she planned a wedding but never showed up to be married. Edie will milk this story dry. Maybe too dry, because Edie does tend to tell a good story often, too often. But this one I'll be glad to hear as many times as she cares to repeat it.

Julia steps into the chamber once more; fragile, she asks, "Where is Edie, Monarose?"

Edie could be anywhere. Locked in a cubicle in the bathroom at Grand Central Station. Perched on top of Mount Fuji with a pair of binoculars, insisting she can see across oceans and continents to the east side of Manhattan. Or she could be in Kabul. From Kabul, a girl can go anywhere. "Kabul," Edie used to dream. "Listen to the sound that makes, Monarose. Kabul. When you get to Kabul, the world is wide open to you." Or Edie might very well be in my apartment, sprawled out on my divan, tapping her fingernails against her teeth, wondering what's taking me so long to get back with the details of the wedding she missed. "Did the groom look miserable?" she'll ask. "Were the guests shocked? Did anyone cry? Did the lilacs rot?"

Employing the use of the cliffhanger, I'll make her wait a moment before saying, "Oh, Edie, you should've been there. It was more fun than Louise Crane's wedding."

And she'll grin and say, "It was a good one, wasn't it? Why, I even had you going, didn't I?"

"Almost," I'll say. "Almost."

150

Julia gathers fortitude, inhaling deeply. "She wouldn't, Monarose? Would she?"

I try to look concerned, grave. "I don't know," I tell Julia. "I really thought she'd be here, but now I just don't know."

"She wouldn't," Julia aims to convince herself. "I'll call her again. Maybe she overslept."

After all these weeks of faking it, my face aches from the pleasure of a smile that's sincere.

In walks Edie. Rather, in runs Edie is more like it. Out of breath, she says, "I can't believe I'm late to my own wedding."

My throat gets tight. Disappointment does not go down any easier the second time around. "We thought you weren't coming," I say.

Edie doesn't answer because Steve walks in, gaseous with relief. He offers Edie a few minutes to get herself together while he goes off to inform her mother, the groom, and the guests that the bride has arrived. Some of the guests just lost their money.

"This must be mine." Edie's at the florist's box. Inside is her bouquet, lilacs and ferns tied together with a chintzy white bow. There is also a sprig of lilacs wired to a bobby pin. "Help me clip this in my hair, will you." Edie hands me the spray of flowers with two additional pins.

I lean close to her. Edie stinks of gin. "Edie," I say. "You're tanked."

"No," she counters. "I'm relaxed."

"Sherry," I tell her, "is for relaxing. Gin is for getting tanked."

"Getting married is nerve-wracking," she says. "You ought to try it sometime."

The lilacs won't stay put in Edie's hair. They, too, rebel at having to be a part of this and slip free each time Edie moves. "You've got to get them to stay," she says. "I want lilacs in my hair. Do something. I want to be a beautiful bride."

I mash a lilac bud between my thumb and forefinger until it's mush. The sap is sticky.

Edie suggests we go to the bathroom. "Maybe we'll have an easier time of it there."

In the ladies' room, Edie goes to the mirror. I sit on the one chair. It's really more of a stool in the corner, cushioned in plastic. I haven't the guts to go to Edie's side. I can look at her from any angle except the one in the mirror, the one reflecting illusions. Edie and I spent so many hours standing side by side before mirrors. Should I ever return to any of them, I'd expect to find our reflections lingering there, sharing a lipstick called Passion Pink. Edie's hair would be longer, and I'd be a bit softer around the edges, but that would be us.

"I can't get these damn lilacs to stay put." Edie hurls the flowers across the room. With her back to me, she says, "I need a cigarette."

I take out two Dunhills and light them. I stand and reach out to pass one to Edie and get caught—freeze-framed—in the mirror. I watch myself hand Edie the cigarette. I watch her reflection watching, too. Images rush by the way your life is reputed to flash before your eyes just as your car plows into a tree. It's an action-packed instant.

Whereas I have given serious consideration to the subject, Edie apparently hadn't thought about having to be tough today. She's not prepared. She takes the cigarette from me and comes apart. Edie is sobbing.

"Don't cry, Edie," I say. "This is the happiest day of your life, remember? You're not supposed to cry on the happiest day of your life."

Between sniffles, Edie says, "This is the happiest day of my life."

"Then quit crying. Brides don't cry," I tell her, very no-nonsense.

Edie cries more. A wrenching cry, heaving and shaking, coming from someplace deep inside, like her liver or kidneys.

"You've got to stop this, Edie. Your makeup's running down your face. You've got goop all over yourself. Now wash up," I instruct.

Only, Edie keeps on crying. I'd like to be able to tell her it's okay to run off if she wants to. It's not too late. She doesn't have to go through with a wedding. Except Edie knows this. Edie's crying because she *doesn't* want to run off.

I turn away and smoke while she cries. After all the lousy days I've had lately, let her be miserable for a change. I'm comfortable with such spitefulness until Edie throws her arms around my neck and cries on my jacket. It's a good thing I wore black, after all.

Edie and I have never hugged before. Not in all the years we've been friends. But here she is now, hugging the breath from me. I don't like it. My arms hang limply at my sides, hoping she'll take the hint and let go of me. When that doesn't happen, I try to hug her back, lifting my arms to a semicircle, but I can't complete the sphere. Finally, I sort of pat her on the shoulder. Edie allows this, which surprises me. I guess I was expecting her to bat my hand away.

This hugging and patting and sniveling is all so feeble. We ought to be smashing mirrors, clogging the sinks, flooding the toilets. Acts of significance. Sternly, to let Edie know this rush of emotion is not quite dignified, I say, "There, there. Pull youself together." I pry her arms away from me and tell her she's got to get a grip on herself. "You've got to go get married," I say.

Edie steps back and nods. She sniffles and smiles with difficulty, as if she's suffering from a particularly bad hangover. I escort her to the sink and turn on the faucet. "Now wash," I say.

There aren't any paper towels here, which somehow fits into the scheme of things. I unroll a wad of toilet paper and give it to Edie to dry her hands and face. "Do I have time to fix my makeup?" she asks.

"Of course you do. You're the bride. They've got to wait for you. Take all the time you want."

Blending her lipstick, Edie turns to me and asks, "Do I look okay?"

"Fine," I tell her. "You look fine."

Edie and I pause, and I say, "Edie?"

"Come on," she says. "I've got to go get married."

Steve is waiting for us in the attendants' chamber with directions for the ceremony. He nods at me and says, "When you see me at the altar, count to five and then slowly walk up the aisle. Slow-ly," he repeats, as if I were a moron. "This is a ceremony. A pageant. When you reach the altar, step three paces off to your left."

The ring Edie's giving Gerald is my responsibility. I'm to hang onto it until the part of the cermony where Steve says, "With this ring." Then I'm to hand it to Edie. She is to take the gold band and vow her life away.

Steve instructs Edie to wait for me to get settled in, count to seven, and begin her march down the aisle. "Remember," Steve tells her, "you're the bride. Give everyone a chance to get a good look at you." Edie is to come to rest on my right.

"You've got that now? Both of you?" Steve doesn't want us screwing up his act.

With everything finally under control, Steve makes his entrance. Edie grabs her bouquet off the table. She grips it with both hands, as if someone were going to try to snatch it from her.

Maybe it's only the lighting here, but Edie doesn't look well. "Are you okay?" I ask. I could swear she's white with a green tint. "The gin's not backing up on you, is it?"

"I'm all right," she says.

At the altar, Steve stands there waiting for the audience to hush. What a ham.

"Edie, you're sure you're okay?"

"Fine," she snaps. "I'm fine."

There isn't any organ music to keep a beat, and Steve did say to take it slow, so I poke up the aisle. Inching my way along, I turn my head left and right in slow motion, like a mechanical doll, scouting the ranks for someone who might spring from his seat as Steve says, "Let him speak now or . . ."

That's my favorite part to any wedding. Guests shift and squirm, awaiting the hero who will pop up from the rear pew professing a far greater love than the groom can offer. If I were ever to marry, I'd definitely want someone there objecting.

In my place at the altar, I face Steve. He's basking in the glow of the footlights. The groom and that excuse for a best man are at my right.

I begin counting to seven but make it only to four when Edie barrels in. She stops short between me and the groom. She faces her husband-to-be. Steve allows this display to get digested before he begins. He's not about to be upstaged. I look up, past the ceiling. For a split second, I think I've got the divine intervention I'd been asking for, but it's only Steve clearing his throat, not the rumbling of thunder.

He begins to read.

I can't really find fault with Shakespeare. I mean, there isn't any bad Shakespeare, but if there were bad Shakespeare, it would have to be the 116th sonnet, the one Steve's reading with an accent which is growing more clipped with each line:

"Let me not to the marriage of true minds
Admit impediment. Love is not love
Which alters when it alteration finds . . ."

A trace of Cockney sneaks in. What a boob.

Withen his bending sickle's compass come.
Love alters not with his brief hours and weeks . . ."

This sonnet is as much a wedding standard as "O Promise Me." A cliché. As long as we've got the volume of Shakespeare handy, we ought to do Ophelia's mad scene. Edie'd be a natural for that, given the circumstances.

"If this be error, and upon me be proved,
I never writ, nor no man ever loved."

Steve takes a barely perceptible bow before moving on with his dirty business. "Dearly beloved, we are gathered together on this day . . ."

I stop listening. Instead, I attempt to transmit brain waves to Edie. I think loudly, with oomph, "RUN! Run for it. Hike up your skirt, Edie, and run before it's too late." I'm banking on our ability to yak with each other telepathically. "Run, Edie. Please, please run."

Edie nudges me with her elbow. She whispers something, but I don't quite catch it.

"What?" I ask.

"The ring. Give me the ring."

I fork over the wedding band. Edie takes it and repeats after Steve, "With this ring, I thee wed." She slides the ring onto Gerald's extended pudgy finger. I think I'm going to be ill.

Not exactly a buzz, but more of a whir hums in my ears. It sounds like the ocean in a conch shell. I strain to listen to it, to hear what the sea anemones and mermaids are saying, but the humming fades as Steve's voice blares in at me, like the sound on a bum television that takes time to warm up. "For better or worse, as long as you both shall live?"

The groom says, "I do."

It's Edie's turn, but she's quiet. There's a moment of silence to hang years on, as if we've all frozen in time, quit breathing, and every clock has ceased to tick, until Edie says, "I do."

And I think, "Well, she's done it."

Despite Steve's direction that we file out the same way we filed in, it doesn't happen. We drift apart, haphazardly disperse, and amble around the chapel.

No one looks any too happy. Not even Edie's mother. The crease in her forehead is deeper than her smile. Nervous as she was that this wedding might not take place,

158

I can't say she looks any too pleased now that it has. Reality has a way of dawning a little past schedule.

Even those who won bets are disgruntled. It was recreational gambling. They'd have preferred a good show. Boys are complaining they had to wear suits. Some have already put their ties in their pockets, having noticed this isn't a special occasion. The losers are paying off their debts.

I slink to a far corner pew and sit. Edie used to tell me the only reality is money, and because money could always be had, reality was no concern of ours. But Edie was wrong about that. Sad realities do happen, but miracles do not.

From the corner of my eye, I see Edie coming toward me. I stand up and step into the aisle to meet her head-on. "Congratulations," I say.

She shrugs. Some strands of hair fall from place and over her eye, cutting across the bridge of her nose. I reach out and fix it for her.

"It's not over," Edie says. "This doesn't change anything. Not really. You mustn't think it's over."

That is just so like Edie to pretend it's not over when it plainly is, when she was the one who caused it to end.

I chew on my lower lip, and as if there were a pane of glass between us, Edie chews on hers. I let my lip go, and so does Edie. She smiles, expecting me to follow her lead, when from across the room, her husband shouts, "Edie! Come here. We're taking pictures now."

Edie turns in the direction of the man she's gone and

married. He's waving her over. She knows she has to go to him, but she hesitates.

"Go on," I tell her. "Go have your picture taken."

"You come, too." Edie takes hold of my arm. "I want a picture of us together."

I pull free of her and take a step back. "You go on," I say. "I'll catch up to you in a minute."

Edie joins her husband. The photographer shuffles the bride and groom around as if they were shills in a three-card monte game. Flashbulbs pop.

Forget what I told Edie. I lied. I'm not about to have my picture taken today. I will not be in her wedding album. And after a lot of years, she'll flip through it, unable to recall if I attended her wedding or not.

I have only one picture of Edie. One that I can hold, one with permanence to it. It was taken before I knew her, when she was fifteen and a blonde. When she gave it to me, I'd looked hard at it and asked, "This is you? Why do you have blonde hair?" Someday, I'll be digging around in my junk and come upon the picture of the blonde girl, and I'll think, "Who the hell is that? That's not anyone I know."

I duck out to the lobby. I can almost hear the bells chime midnight, so clear it is to me that it's well time for me to leave the ball, that my coach has turned back into a pumpkin hooked up to mice and rats, that there is no more fairy godmother making magic. After smoking half of a cigarette, I drop the remains on the floor. I don't bother crushing it with my shoe and, like all things, it burns itself out.

160

The chapel doors swing open. The wedding party empties into the lobby, swarming around the newlyweds. This is my cue. I fish around in my purse for the handkerchief filled with rice. The knot I'd made is tight, and before I manage to get it open, hoots and giggles ring out. I look up. A whole bunch of people, Edie's mother, some cousins, are tossing rice. Even Henry Cosgrove takes a handful from his pocket, although he misses Edie by five yards. Edie's acting as if she were trying to duck this shower. Her head is bent and she lifts her arm to deflect the spray. Rice lands in her hair, and she's laughing.

I slip the pouch of rice back into my purse.

No one here dives to catch Edie's bouquet. Rather, as if it were tainted, jinxed, we clear away from it. Her lilacs land on the floor. The best man takes a step forward and flattens the bow with his heel.

EPILOGUE

The sun is high, but westerly, in preparation for dusk. The wedding party breaks into clusters along the way to the reception. We're supposed to go eat, drink, and make merry in one of those penthouse restaurants which were all the rage until word leaked out their food was boiled in a baggie.

As the others round the corner, I hold back and shoulder myself against the brick of an apartment house. Pinned to the wall like a spy or a fugitive, I periodically peer around the bend to watch Edie and Gerald and family and friends grow smaller in the distance. When I can no longer see them at all, I cross the street.

With fast steps, I hurry until I hit Fifth Avenue. There

I slow down to an easy stroll because that is the nature of walking on Fifth. Strolling. Window shopping. Scouting for boys and baubles. Straw hats with grosgrain ribbons trailing down girls' backs. A light breeze tickles at my legs.

A big crowd is gathered on the steps of Saint Patrick's Cathedral. It is not the lunchtime crowd drinking soda, eating yogurt. This crowd is dressed to the nines. I go over and blend in with them just as a bride and groom emerge from the cathedral doors. They seem like a nice couple. The crowd cheers, claps, whistles, makes rodeo noises, but no one tosses rice. They have all forgotten to bring rice to toss.

As the bride passes me, I sprinkle Edie's rice over her. She stops, glad someone was so thoughtful. I have a hunch no one remembered to give her something old either, so I press the silk handkerchief to her hand. She must be thinking I'm from the groom's side of the family, a cousin she could grow fond of, be friends with.

At the limousine waiting to whisk the couple away, the bride prepares to throw her bouquet. The brides-maids clamor and jostle for a good position. The bride gives me a wink, but I don't want to catch the jonquils and baby's breath. I duck behind a beefy bridesmaid in a full taffeta dress. The beefy girl makes the catch and holds up her prize.

Along with the other well-wishers, I wave the bride and groom off. Although I'm quite sure I'd be most wel-come at their reception, I continue on my way.

The Plaza Hotel looms large in my view. Its stature

takes command, diminishes whatever else might be in sight. I don't want to go inside, but I cross over to the fountain and sit, Dale Evans sidesaddle, on the edge. I face the park where the hansom cabs are lined up.

During the winter, the fountain is dry. Otherwise it might turn to ice and crack. Often in the heat of summer it's dry, too. This has to do either with water conservation or the worry that unimaginative types, unable to come up with an original stunt, will dip in it. But today the fountain sprouts and gurgles. The pool is filled.

Pennies, nickels, and dimes dot the bottom, distorted by the water's movement, like a mirror in a fun house. Silly people threw bits of money away. Still—it strikes me as curious—there aren't any quarters down there. Nor silver dollars. Ten cents a dream? But not worth a buck? Maybe that's why wishes don't come true. The offerings are too chintzy. If you're not willing to risk more than loose change, then how significant was the depth of your desire?

I catch my reflection in the pool. What a sap I am, sitting on the fountain's edge, gazing forlornly at myself. If this were some crummy foreign movie, now would be the part where a dapper man approaches me. He'd stare at me, not a once-over, but a long, meaningful stare, laden with sensitivities. His eyes would be big, soft, and brown. He'd be wearing Gucci loafers. "Madame," he'd say, "pourquoi you look so sad?" His voice and mouth movements would be out of synch.

That would be my movie. Edie wouldn't be in it. Just me and the dapper man and a cast of thousands I haven't yet met. I guess that's what happens when you start out telling someone else's story; you wind up telling your own.

And when you know that, that it is your story, you quit wallowing in self-pity. You hold your head up. You chew yourself out just as you would some sot in a bar crying into his beer. "Quit that sniveling," you say.

From my wallet, I take a twenty-dollar bill and drop it into the fountain. Paper money doesn't sink fast the way coins do. Like a sailboat overturned on a lake, the twenty-dollar bill floats, and I've got ample time to wish.